The
Inferno

Books by Fred Hoyle

THE BLACK CLOUD
FRONTIERS OF ASTRONOMY
GALAXIES, NUCLEI AND QUASARS
THE NATURE OF THE UNIVERSE
OCTOBER THE FIRST IS TOO LATE

Books by Fred and Geoffrey Hoyle

THE MOLECULE MEN
ROCKETS IN URSA MAJOR
SEVEN STEPS TO THE SUN
THE INFERNO

The Inferno

FRED HOYLE

GEOFFREY HOYLE

HARPER & ROW, PUBLISHERS
New York, Evanston, San Francisco, London

Library of Congress Cataloging in Publication Data

Hoyle, Fred.
    The inferno.
    I. Hoyle, Geoffrey, joint author. II. Title.
PZ4.H867In3   [PR6058.098]   823'.9'14
ISBN   0-06-011987-X   73-4151

The
Inferno

1

London

Cameron kissed his wife, Madeleine, good-bye. She leaned out of the train window toward him.

"Phone me and I'll meet you," she said.

"It's hardly worth it."

The train was moving out, slowly at first, no more than walking pace, and then picking up speed. Cameron hoped he'd be doing the same thing himself the following day, or the day after, or . . . He hated waiting around in London, especially for indefinite Whitehall situations. But he'd have to stick it out. He glanced at his watch—7:35 P.M.—and wondered why the government wasn't making time decimal.

Now what to do about dinner? According to the form book he ought to be dining out with some influential person. But who was influential? He decided on Wheeler's in Old Compton Street, took the tube to Leicester Square and walked from there.

An hour and a half later, dinner over, he set off walking again, out along Shaftesbury Avenue, Piccadilly Circus, Lower Regent Street, into Carlton House Terrace. At Number 6 he pressed the "Night Porter" button, announced himself into a small microphone and opened the door as soon as the electrically operated lock came free.

He could sleep like a log in the countryside, especially out of doors, but sleep never came easily in big cities and he wondered how he would fare tonight. The Royal Society, here in Carlton House Terrace, was commendably far from the heavy traffic. Even so he could hear a general outside hum.

But he woke only once during the night. The hum outside was almost gone. Ridiculously, he found himself listening for it. Then somehow he was asleep again, until the housekeeper brought his breakfast at 8 A.M. sharp. He ate the roll and croissant slowly, dabbing bits of marmalade on the pieces as he broke them with his hands. He wondered what the day would bring. More delay—that was a safe enough bet. He had until 11 A.M. to kill. After packing his bag, he paid the housekeeper and walked the few yards to the Athenaeum Club. Here he filled in the time by reading the morning papers. Someone in the U.S. had discovered an x-ray pulsar. Few readers of the *Times*, he decided, would share his view that this was the only significant news.

A little after ten-thirty he set off down the long flight of stone steps into The Mall, turning left to Trafalgar Square and into Whitehall, arriving at his destination in Richmond Terrace a few minutes before eleven. As always, walking into the Department of Education and Science, he was depressed by its dismal shabbiness—which could only be a matter of deliberate policy. He was shown into the office of Sir Henry Mallinson, First Secretary.

Mallinson and Cameron had both been at Pembroke, Cambridge. Mallinson had been one year senior. They had known each other reasonably well as students, playing Rugby together in the College first fifteen. After their student days they had seen nothing of each other for many years, until Mallinson was moved from Mintech to DES and Cameron was appointed to head the new accelerator project at CERN, Geneva, the European Center for Nuclear Research. As the British subscription to CERN was channeled through DES, the connection was now quite close. It is an odd aspect of middle age, the tie that binds men—or women—who have been students together, the unspoken tie, superficially fragile, yet with a curious strength which others can never share.

"Coffee?" said Mallinson. "It's white, isn't it?"

"Please."

"Did you have a good trip over?"

"Yes. Madeleine came with me."

"Shopping trip?"

"No; I'm hoping to take a few days' leave before going back. Up in the Highlands."

"You've got a place up there, haven't you?"

"Yes, Kintail."

"Road to Skye?"

"Thank goodness, no. On the lochside—to the south. You branch off the Glenelg road."

"I know it. Fine spot."

"Yes, the loch comes to the bottom of the garden."

"Lucky. I'm stuck in London, I'm afraid."

"Isn't it time for some departments to move out?"

"Everybody keeps on saying so. By the way, we're lunching with the Minister."

"Glad you told me."

"It was last-minute."

"Crisis?"

"Not really."

Mallinson grinned across his desk. "I'd guess it depended on how things have been going. In the Cabinet."

"Has the mountain labored?"

"If by that you mean has a decision been reached, the answer is yes."

Cameron finished his coffee with restrained slowness. By rights he should have been nervy, but he'd known from the first

3

moment he'd seen Mallinson's face. He'd known the decision had to be favorable. Over the past couple of months the scientific world had expected the British government to come down at last in favor of proceeding with plans for the vast new 1000-Gev machine at Geneva. It would be a five to ten years' job, which meant it would probably be the last big one that Cameron himself would ever tackle. But this was the way he wanted it. When he'd started after the war as a junior member of the team that built the first British Gev machine, he'd thought it a great thing. He'd progressed in thirty years from 1 Gev to 1000 Gev. This was a fair enough achievement for a lifetime's work. After that he'd be content to leave physics to younger men, especially as the bigger half of the problem nowadays was political and financial rather than scientific.

"And the answer is . . . ?"

"A bit of a relief for you. We've got the green light—or at least we're going to get it. It's confidential still."

"Which means it's not for *Nature*, I suppose."

"That's right."

"Why keep a decision confidential if it's already been taken?"

"Possible complications. There's a condition to it."

"Condition?"

"That all the present adherents join."

Cameron felt the pressure building up now. By all the adherents Mallinson obviously meant all the countries at present contributing to CERN. But Cameron knew there were genuine doubts about one or two of the smaller ones.

"So, if Denmark says no, we say no?" he burst out.

"Officially that's the position."

"But it's ridiculous!" Cameron was angry now.

"No, it's not. It's a nuisance but it's not ridiculous."

"What the devil does it matter what one or two of the smaller countries wish to do?"

"It doesn't matter. But it *does* matter what the Germans and the French do."

4

"We know what they want to do. They want to go ahead. They've been saying so for more than a year."

"Unofficially."

"At ministerial level, if you call that unofficial."

Mallinson smiled with mock weariness.

"My dear chap, what is said is one thing—even if it is said at ministerial level. What is signed is another thing. Once the Germans and the French come in officially, we come in officially."

"Irrespective of Denmark?"

"Irrespective of any of the smaller contributors."

"Then why the devil not say so?"

"Because it isn't on politically to start drawing categories. We cannot say openly that France is important but that Switzerland isn't. Obviously. But we can always change our conditions once the big fish commit themselves."

Cameron was red with anger now. He found it impossible to contain himself. Jumping from his chair, he took the center of the room, exclaiming in an anguished voice, "But it means *delay*. More *delay*. We've been delaying now for three years."

"I wouldn't have said it was at all bad. Three years isn't long for a fifty-million project. Fielding waited the best part of ten years for his radiotelescope."

"Which is nothing to boast about. If Fielding had got the telescope ten years ago he'd have had ten years' work done with it by now."

"And been asking for another one."

"In any case, this isn't a national affair, it's international."

"If it wasn't international you wouldn't be getting fifty million."

Cameron subsided back into the chair.

"I suppose not," he conceded.

Mallinson was still smiling.

"In any case, it will give you time for going up to Scotland, won't it?"

"It's not a joking matter, Henry. Keeping a team together with everybody keen and raring to go becomes impossible with all these delays and uncertainties. One long delay to begin with —everybody can understand that. It's all the subsidiary delays— three months here, three months there—that knock the devil out of people. What you fellows in the Civil Service never seem to understand is that projects aren't finished once the light goes green. They may be finished for you but they're only just *beginning* for us. We still have to summon up the energy to drive them through."

"When you get involved on a big scale, things do go slowly. You've got to accept it. Even on a national scale things move slowly. For stability they've got to move slowly. Internationally, it's worse. It isn't our fault in government that physics has got so big. It's just your bad luck."

"I can't help feeling the country would be a lot better off if it made up its mind what it wanted to do and simply did it. Instead of this endless shilly-shallying. I'm not talking about physics now."

"I gather not, which makes what you say less to the point— if I may say so."

Mallinson stood up. "We should be on our way," he went on. "Lunch is twelve forty-five for one o'clock."

Cameron glanced at his watch. It was only a minute or two after twelve.

"We're lunching at Kenyons. It means getting across town."

"Can I ask your secretary to make a call for me?"

"Certainly. But if it's not urgent you could wait till we get back."

"Back?"

"I rather fancy we'll have other things to talk about."

The two men walked from Richmond Terrace to Trafalgar Square, Mallinson dressed in familiar Whitehall style—differing from the men of the City a mile or so to the east in that he carried no telltale umbrella and his hat breathed a suggestion of originality—Cameron, a full six inches the taller, darker in countenance from the hotter sun of Geneva and from days spent on alpine snowfields, without hat and carrying his raincoat. They hailed a taxi, reaching the restaurant just before twelve-thirty.

"Trouble with this damn city," grunted Cameron, "is that if you don't want to be late you have to be early."

Mallinson, as usual, refused to rise to the bait. "There's no demerit in that. We can have an early drink," he remarked with satisfaction.

Cameron was surprised to see the lunch table laid for about twelve. He'd rather expected this would be an intimate affair, just three or four of them. Then it struck him that no conversation with your neighbor can be considered private when as many as four or even six people sit down together. Yet when the number rises to ten or more the conversation fragments, the sound level rises, and you find yourself talking to your immediate neighbor—whether to the right or left—essentially as if the rest of the world did not exist. In fact the safest place for a private conversation was between neighbors at a large formal dinner, since the exceedingly high general noise level makes eavesdropping impossible.

Mallinson tapped him on the shoulder, to inform him that the Secretary of State had arrived. They were introduced, shook hands and, after a short interchange of conventionalities, were seated, with Cameron on the Minister's right.

"Henry Mallinson will have told you the news," the Minister began.

"Yes, I'm very pleased."

Cameron doubted if there was any point in bringing up the question of delay. He had enough understanding of politics to know it is useless to lose time and energy fighting issues that cannot possibly be won. Lost causes do not change the world.

"You don't sound as enthusiastic as I expected," went on the Minister.

"I'm thinking of all the work that has to be done now. Spending money on a big scale isn't easy."

"You know it would make my job easier—talking to the Cabinet—if I could really understand what you physics people are up to. Why d'you want this thing? I know you keep talking about the laws of physics, but the laws of physics don't mean much to the man in the street."

"There's a basic contradiction, isn't there, Minister?"

"In what way?"

"Well, we're all being carried along in the river of life. It's the same for the Cabinet, for the man in the street, for the physicist. As a politician you spend yourself navigating around rocks in the riverbed. But the scientist says to himself: Why am I in this river? What is it anyway? Where has it come from? Where is it going to?"

"But what's the use of asking questions like that if you're heading slapbang for rapids ahead?"

"No use at all. But then I might say: What's the use of everybody trying to pilot the boat? That's just about the quickest way to disaster."

"So you're telling me it takes all sorts to make a world?"

"Yes."

"But if I try to look at things from your point of view I ask myself: Why is it so important to carry out these experiments? I've read as best I can about this thing—what is it, magnetic something or other?"

"Magnetic moment."

"That's right—magnetic moment—and about time asymmetry. I accept that it's hard to see the importance of this kind of thing from my position. What I'm trying to understand is why it's important from your position."

Cameron thought for a moment before replying.

"Each item of discovery is not crucially important in itself," he began. "If you seek something specially critical in any discovery—like the magnetic moment of the muon being the same as the electron—well, you're looking in the wrong place."

"How d'you mean looking in the wrong place?"

"I mean it isn't so much the item of discovery that is important in itself as the process of discovery. Some things about the world we see clearly. Other things we see indistinctly through a veil. Still other things lie in shadow, completely hidden. It is the process of wrenching the veil apart which is of true importance to the scientist. The thrill—if you like to call it that—lies in seeing something for the first time."

"Like walking on the moon for the first time."

"Yes, or like climbing a mountain for the first time. It is the irresistible urge to find out what lies beyond."

"Yet you wouldn't set as great a store by walking on the moon as you would by discovering some new physical law?"

"No, I wouldn't."

"Why?"

"Because a new law would mean a big area of new territory still to be explored. To use a mundane analogy, it would be like the difference between a vast oil strike and a comparatively small one."

Cameron was suddenly aware that somehow he had contrived to eat his lunch without noticing it. Henry Mallinson was there standing behind his chair.

"Ah, Henry is reminding me that we have work to do," the Minister remarked. "I think he has some other things to talk to you about."

"Other things?"

"Yes, the world isn't all made up of nuclear accelerators."

Cameron remembered Mallinson saying something along the same lines. He bade good-bye to the Minister, wondering what might be afoot, and indeed wondering just what the point of the lunch had been.

"You made a great impression on the Minister," Mallinson

remarked as he and Cameron walked back along Whitehall.

"Is that good?"

"Can't do any harm. What was the topic, if I may ask?"

" 'Philosophy and the Physicist,' I suppose."

"You found him genuinely interested?"

"Yes, I think so. But what was all this about other things?"

"Let's wait till we get back to the office."

"What was the point of the lunch? if I might ask."

"I thought the two of you should meet."

"And you wanted to impress on me that these 'other things' have importance at ministerial level?"

"A little of that too," admitted Mallinson as they turned into Richmond Terrace.

Cameron spent a few minutes arranging with Mallinson's secretary to send a telex to Geneva and to phone a message through to Madeleine. With this done, he rejoined Mallinson.

"Well, what is it, Henry?" he asked.

"We're in a spot of trouble. You probably don't know it but we're building a large dish—two hundred feet—for microwave radio work. We're building it jointly with the Australians."

"I heard something about it. What order of job is it?"

"Something like two million."

"Each."

"No, one each. Not big by your standard."

"How can you get into trouble with a thing like that?"

Cameron had the air of a man talking about a fly swatter.

"Let me fill you in a bit on the details. Our first idea was to build something smaller, one hundred fifty feet. We were going to do the thing alone. Now the essential point is this—we can't put equipment for this sort of very short radio wavelength in this country. Because of the atmosphere—too much water."

"I can well imagine it."

"Well, we thought about Spain and about the Canary Isles, Tenerife particularly."

"Very nice."

"Unfortunately it wasn't. The sky turned out to be noisy—I believe that is the technical term for it. Just about the time we were discovering that Tenerife was unsuitable, the Australians came forward with a proposition for a joint telescope."

"In Australia?"

"Yes. They produced a lot of data to show how good the Australian sites are. Well, to cut a long story short, it seemed a good way out of our difficulty. And with two countries chipping in funds, we were able to upgrade the size of the dish."

"I see, from one hundred fifty feet to two hundred?"

"That's right. Well, when I say we've got trouble on our hands—"

"You mean you've got trouble with the Aussies." Cameron grinned.

"You know about it?" Mallinson's eyebrows were raised.

"Of course not. But there are two kinds of trouble, personal and technical. You'd hardly be concerned with a technical problem, would you, Henry?"

"Quite right, I wouldn't. But in a sense the difference *is* technical, which is where you come into the picture, my boy."

"I'm damned if I'm going to act as a nursemaid, especially for astronomers."

"Why especially?"

"They're a quarrelsome lot, notoriously. I'm not getting involved with their kind of nonsense."

"Wait! Wait!"

Mallinson leaned back in his chair, his hands raised high in the air.

"What is there to wait for?"

"Just let me go on with my story."

"If you must."

"You can imagine this dish has to be made with great accuracy."

"I can."

"The bone of contention is how the necessary accuracy is to be achieved, no more than a fraction of a millimeter error in two hundred feet."

"How are they proposing to do it?"

"Our people want a fairly rigid kind of structure but with a movable skin."

"Movable?"

"Jacking points which are adjustable."

"You mean a feedback system—variable adjustment to get the right shape?"

"That's the kind of idea. I'm not a technical expert, so I only understand it in a general sort of way."

"I still don't see . . ."

"The trouble is the Australians want an automatically deformable structure, a structure designed to maintain its shape at all orientations. As I understand it, the thing is supposed to flow into itself."

"I'm with you. They're known as homologously deforming structures."

"Ah, you know about them. Good."

"Just where do you come into this thing, Henry? I'd have thought it was a severely technical problem."

"I come into it because the split is unfortunately on national lines. If there were some Australians and some British on each side I wouldn't give a damn about it. Except to want a proper solution, of course."

"I see. It's the political aspect of the problem?"

"Exactly. We don't want it to escalate."

"Suppose you tell me what you propose to do."

"We've agreed—"

"Who is we?"

"This office in the U.K. My opposite number in Australia."

"And what have you agreed?"

"We've agreed to appoint two uncommitted experts, one from each side."

"I see, arbitration. With me as your expert. Is that it?"

"That is it, exactly."

"Send Fielding. Or is he involved already? I'd have thought with that great telescope up at Pitlochry he'd have more on his hands than—"

"Fielding is a British radioastronomer. He could hardly do anything except support the position of his colleagues."

"You don't want me to support it?"

"I don't give a damn whether you support it or not, as long as you sort things out in a mutually acceptable way."

"Look, Henry, this is ridiculous. I haven't any experience of radiotelescopes."

"Which is exactly why I'm asking you to step in. You have experience in handling large projects, projects much bigger than this one, projects demanding even greater accuracy of detail. You understand contractual work. You are an internationally respected scientist. In Australian eyes you are uncommitted. They will accept your position in good faith. There is no one remotely as suitable as you are."

"Let me remind you that I do have other work."

"Accepted. You have work much more important than this. Accepted. But that work is subject to something like three months' delay. Oh, no! Don't blame me...."

Cameron had half risen from his chair at the mention of delay.

"I'm not that devious a chap," concluded Mallinson.

Cameron spoke swiftly, as he always did. It wasn't his way to prevaricate. "I'd need to think about it. I'll let you know—well, within a few days."

"Reasonable." Mallinson nodded. "Here," he went on, picking up a stack of papers, "are the technicalities. You'll need them. I can't understand them, but you can."

"I'm taking a week's leave."

"Something to occupy your mind in the evenings," came Mallinson's imperturbable reply as he handed the papers to Cameron. "How are you going up?" he asked, with the air of having reached a satisfactory conclusion.

"Train."

"Night train?"

"Yes, more convenient than a flight. At this time of day."

Mallinson took the hint. "I'm sorry for the delay, my dear Cameron, but it's a more important business than the money might suggest. And don't forget—you *are* getting fifty million out of us."

2

Scotland: October

Cameron finished his breakfast as the Highland Flier ground its way up the long incline from Tyndrum to Gorton Siding. He decided there was little point in returning from the dining carriage to his sleeper, at any rate until the train reached Loch Treig. He sat looking out over the wilderness of Rannoch Moor, wondering if technology would ever reach the stage of being able to "develop" such intractable country. He hoped profoundly that it wouldn't. He also wondered, as he frequently did, how he would feel about living permanently back in the Highlands.

There was an early-morning mist lying here and there in pockets. For all that, Cameron had the feeling the day was going to be fine. After Corrour, the train picked up speed in the long descent to Spean Bridge. Cameron paid his bill and returned to the sleeper to pack his bag. There was still plenty of time but there was no point in rushing at the last moment.

Madeleine was waiting with the car at Spean Bridge. It was still only 9 A.M., so she must have started from Kintail not much after 7 A.M. He'd expected she would be there, because Madeleine always liked to be punctual. He'd also expected to find Pancho, the big white Pyrenean mountain dog, sprawled over the back seat of the car. But there was no sign of Pancho.

"Where's Pancho?" he asked.

Madeleine's face puckered up the way it always did when she was about to burst into tears.

"You'd better let me drive," he went on.

Because of his uneasy overnight journey, he'd intended at first that Madeleine should drive, but it would be better to have the scene out on the road rather than here in the station yard.

British quarantine restrictions for dogs are so strict that they had decided a year ago not to take Pancho with them to Geneva. Once out of the country, it would have been well nigh impossible to get him back in again. The dog had been left with Duncan Fraser, a neighbor in Kintail. When they were on the main road to Invergarry, going up the incline towards the War Memorial, Cameron asked.

"What happened?"

"He got away," blurted Madeleine through her handkerchief.

"Away?"

"Duncan says he cleared a high fence—it must be fully eight feet. Probably in the early morning."

"When did this happen?"

"About three months ago."

"Surely he must have been found?"

"They were hoping to find him. That's why Duncan says he didn't write."

Cameron knew the big dog would take easily to life on the hills. It had the instincts of a wild creature pretty fully developed. In fact it was only the tie with himself and Madeleine which had kept the creature domesticated. With the two of them away, it was no wonder the dog had made a burst for freedom.

"We'll find him soon enough," he asserted.

Now Madeleine was sobbing in earnest.

"We won't," she gulped. "He was shot last week."

16

"Who did it?"

"Some farmer, over in Strathfarrar. They say he was worrying the sheep."

Cameron drove on for several miles, until he was recovered enough to be surprised at the intensity of his anger. His first impulse had been to break the bastard's gun over his head, and perhaps a good deal besides. It was an impulse belonging two hundred years in the past, to the days when a dog could not be shot with impunity if it happened to be owned by a powerful clansman. Cameron was analytical enough to understand the wellspring of his rage. Nowadays all the farmer need do was to claim the dog had been sheep-worrying, and his word would be accepted in law. Besides, Pancho might have been going for the sheep, after running wild for three months. Thinking it would be better to cool off for a day or two before having it out with the fellow, Cameron turned off the Inverness road at Invergarry. As they swept past the side turning to Tomdoun he broke his long reflective silence.

"It looks as though I might have to go to Australia."

In surprise, Madeleine stopped sniffing. "I thought it was urgent to get back to Geneva."

"There's going to be another delay. Probably three months."

By the time he had finished explaining the situation they were at Shiel. Taking the Glenelg road first, and then turning right onto the Letterfearn side road along the south shore of Loch Duich, they reached home at about eleven. The house was of Canadian timber. It fitted snugly against the hillside about a mile short of Totaig.

It had been a matter of some judgment to decide between extensive modifications to a traditional stone cottage and the possibility of importing a new house in a new style. This was at a time when Cameron had been working in the U.K., at a time when he could reach the Highlands much more readily and more frequently than he could now from Geneva. He'd wanted a place where he could both relax and work in some comfort—which meant modern conveniences. So he and Madeleine had decided in favor of the Canadian house, comfortably central-heated with gas delivered from Inverness in enormous cylinders.

"I think you should have an hour or two in bed. I don't suppose you slept much last night," said Madeleine, once they had unpacked the car and set the coffee percolator going.

"Later maybe. I'm going round to have a word with Duncan Fraser."

They drank the coffee in silence, gazing out over the loch through a large window. At high tide the water came almost up to the lawn at the bottom of the garden, where a twelve-foot boat had been beached.

"I would not have thought it was possible for him to get over there," said Duncan Fraser, for perhaps the tenth time. He and Cameron stood in front of a high wire fence, gazing up to the top of it.

"It's no fault of yours, Duncan."

"I should not have let it happen, though."

Indeed it was no fault of Duncan's. Even Cameron, knowing the enormous strength of the dog, would not have thought it possible for him to have clawed his way upward to such a height. Only a desperate and furious desire to escape could have impelled him to such frantic effort.

"It was early in the day?"

"Aye; he was away onto the hill by the time we were about," answered Duncan.

"Ah, well. I'll have something to say in Strathfarrar."

"There's no satisfaction to be had from those people."

"No, when anyone, or anything, is dead, there's never any satisfaction, Duncan. *But I'll be expressing an opinion,*" Cameron concluded in Gaelic.

"*It is a shame that opinions are only spoken.*"

"*A shame indeed.*" Cameron stood rocking on his heels, staring away out over the loch, a strongly built man, his dark hair silvered now at the temples. He sucked air through his teeth and mentally cursed the niceties of a democratic age.

"There's a fair chance that I'll be back for Christmas, Duncan. I was wondering if I could get a couple of loads of wood. It'll be as well to lay it by now."

"Aye, I can do that for you, Mr. Cameron. There's no need to trouble yourself."

"It's trouble for you."

"Not at all. It's only an odd hour with the tractor."

"It's very kind of you, Duncan."

"Not at all, Mr. Cameron."

Duncan was still feeling guilty about the dog. Cameron knew he would regain composure by handling the wood, such a strange tangle are human emotions.

Back at the house, Cameron tried to make up his mind between spending the afternoon out on the loch doing a spot of fishing or browsing through the papers which Mallinson had given him. In the end he simply fell asleep. Waking an hour before dinner, he began chiding himself, but Madeleine would have none of it.

"You've been at full stretch now for six months or more. You need a rest, doing absolutely nothing."

Cameron growled that doing absolutely nothing wasn't his idea of a rest—it was his idea of purgatory. Yet after dinner he soon was feeling sleepy again and so was away early to bed.

Energy returned the following morning. He was up early, cooked himself bacon and eggs, took Madeleine a couple of pieces of toast and a pot of tea, and then stepped outside to sniff the air. There was an October nip to it but the day was going to be clear and bright. The only question to decide was whether to launch the boat or to get out his boots and make for the hills. The chill nip decided him in favor of the mountains. It was a day to keep moving.

He told Madeleine to expect him back probably between four and five, and was soon away in the car. By the time he reached Shiel Bridge he'd decided in favor of the Saddle, in preference to the Five Sisters Ridge. And a· mile or two up Glen Shiel he parked the car, having decided to go for the Forcan Ridge. It was steep and spectacular but no more than a straightforward scramble.

Cameron started at a smooth pace up a zigzag track. The Pancho affair had upset him, but not because of a particular sentiment for the dog. It was true that he and Madeleine, being childless, were probably more attached to it than a larger family would be. Yet it wasn't this either. It was rather that he was suddenly aware of the evanescence of all life. Birth, growing up, struggling— whether for survival or for excellence of achievement—and then death. The pattern was always the same. From the point of view of the individial, the story was always and inevitably one of tragedy. Yet from the point of view of life in the abstract, it was simply a matter of permuting and combining the same materials in a bewildering variety of forms, now as a blade of grass, a tree, a dog, a sheep, a human. The same stuff going endlessly round and round.

These thoughts were interrupted by shouts from away to Cameron's left. Jerked back to an awareness of his surroundings, he realized he must have climbed about six hundred feet above the road. Some three hundred yards away was a party of five or six, stalking obviously. The glint of sunlight on the barrels of their rifles made their purpose plain enough: to reduce the margin of life over death. Two of the party, the gillies, one an older man—older than Cameron—the other some twenty years younger, moved purposefully across his path.

"Where d'ye think ye're going?" asked the older man with little ceremony.

"I think I'm going exactly where I have a mind to be going."

"And that will be back to the road."

Yesterday Cameron had been furiously angry at the shooting of his dog. The same rage now focused on these men, these scavengers who would now be shooting the deer. No doubt in academic debate it would be argued that the deer had to be "kept down." Kept down to a few thousands in the interests of man. Man, who deemed it his right to overpopulate the earth in his grotesque thousands of millions. It was man who needed to be "kept down," not the deer, not the sheep, not the birds, nor his dog Pancho. It was this appalling creature man who deemed it his sacred right to keep himself alive at all costs and who then proceeded ruthlessly to thin out—to cull, as these "sportsmen" called it—the other animals.

"*What manner of vermin are you to be the lackeys of men of the south?*" asked Cameron of the gillies.

The Gaelic took them by surprise. They looked Cameron over with wary suspicion and then fell back several paces when they recognized him. They recognized him not at all as a physicist of international reputation, but as a descendant of the Cameron of the '45.

"*It is our job, sir. There is little enough to be done in these valleys in this time,*" explained the older man.

"*What are we to be telling them, sir?*" asked the younger one with a jerk of his head toward his employers.

"*Tell them they walk on the bones of my ancestors.*"

One of the employers, whether on long- or short-term rental Cameron didn't know, or perhaps one of these self-styled modern "owners," left the others and began moving across the hillside with the plain intention of disposing of any argument which might be developing between Cameron and the gillies. Cameron decided he would see the fellow off the hills, him and his party, down to the road and out of the valley—self-styled landowner or not. He knew who the gillies would elect to follow when the pinch came. But the gillies read the expression on his face, and indeed there was no mistaking its baleful significance. Intent now on avoiding a crisis, they touched their hats at Cameron and moved quickly away to intercept their employer. Cameron watched the three men in conversation for the best part of ten minutes. Then they turned away, leaving him to resume his climb up the rough mountainside.

It wasn't long before remorse came on him. The past was one thing, loyalty to the past was one thing, but the modern truth of it was that these men had perforce to seek employment in this way if they were to continue living in the homes of their forefathers. By his action he was in fact aiding and abetting those who had destroyed the ancient way of life. Cameron realized that he was coming to behave, during his infrequent visits to the Highlands, more and more like a hereditary chieftain. It was something which had grown strongly on him in recent years. Either he must keep away from the Highlands altogether—if only to be fair to the people—or he must return to the Highlands for good and all. His present ambivalence was bad.

These thoughts evaporated from his mind as the ground steepened. It always happened like this. Up to a certain gradient he would turn problems over in his mind. Then the thoughts would disappear and his attention would be wholly occupied in deciding where to go and what places he should put his feet on. Indeed on very steep ground it was impossible to think about anything except the details of the next fifty feet. So it was now on the rocky section of the Forcan Ridge.

By the time he had scrambled over the last pinnacles his subconscious analysis of the problem was complete. He flung himself down by the summit cairn of the Saddle, unpacked a loaf and a hunk of meat, and fully confirmed his intention to complete the new accelerator at Geneva. After .that he was through. He was coming back here, back home to the Highlands. This was the way it was going to be. With his back to a rock, he gazed to the south toward Sgurr na Ciche. Was there anything new and different to be done with this country? he wondered. He remembered a farmer near Quoich Bridge had given up the sheep and had gone back to the old cattle. Back to the past. But what of the future?

A sudden chill in the wind made him polish off the last of his lunch at good speed. Then he was away down to the Bealach to the southeast. His first intention had been to drop immediately from the Bealach back to the road. Then he had a sudden urge to keep going on the far side of the pass, since it occurred to him that he had never been on Faochag, the sugar-loaf mountain which shows up so prominently from the Shiel valley. He was surprised to find the top running quite flat for about half a mile. Unlike the hard stony summit of the Saddle, the ground was soft here with thick turf. Soon he was overlooking Glen Shiel. The descent, although steep, was still soft and smooth, much smoother, in fact, than the way down from the Bealach would have been. He was back at the car in less than an hour from the top of Faochag, which pleased him as demonstrating a fair turn of speed. It wasn't until he had turned the car and was on the way back to Shiel Bridge that he remembered the stalking party. He made a mental note to find out who the gillies were.

3

South Via Strathfarrar

The weather worsened the following day. Madeleine decided to take the car to Inverness, saying that if they were to spend Christmas at the house then she'd better start stocking up the deep freeze. Duncan Fraser delivered the two loads of wood. Cameron had a call from London. Mallinson's office wanted to know urgently when he would be returning south. Thinking there might be further news about the accelerator, Cameron tried to contact Mallinson himself, but was told that he would be tied up all day in a series of meetings. Cursing the uncertainty, Cameron did what he could to read through the radio-telescope material that Mallinson had given him. He sat in front of the big window that opened onto the loch. A fierce wind was whipping the water into short, steep waves. He found it hard to concentrate. Yesterday's exercise made him lethargic. Twice he brewed himself a pot of coffee.

The trouble with Mallinson's documentation was that instead of being an objective account of the two methods of telescope construction, it was in fact undisguised propaganda for the British point of view. The case for the rigid structure was made to appear so overwhelming, the homologously deformable possibility being dealt with so curiously, that Cameron found himself leaning almost automatically toward the Australian point of view, more or less by way of compensation. He wondered if he should go back to Geneva before going to Australia, but decided instead to write a couple of letters, one to his secretary, the other to his second in command. Before he had finished, Madeleine was back.

"I've had London on the phone."

"Can't they leave you alone, even for a couple of days?"

"Apparently not."

"What did they want?"

"They didn't say. Except to find out when we were returning."

Madeleine made a wry face.

"I'd like to leave early, actually. To visit Pitlochry," explained Cameron cryptically.

"Why Pitlochry?"

"The big radiotelescope there. I'd like to see it and talk to the people there."

"When?"

"Let's see how the weather behaves. If it stays bad we could drive over tomorrow. Then I could go on to London by train."

"Leaving me to bring the car back here?"

"Yes."

"Thank you very much."

"Well, you don't want to go to Australia, do you?"

"It depends on how long you'll be there."

"About ten days, I suppose."

Madeleine thought for a moment. Then she shook her head.

"It's hardly worth it, is it? I mean you just about get adjusted and then it's time to come back."

"I don't see how I can be away from Geneva for much longer than that."

"So I'm supposed to stay here."

"Or go back to Geneva."

"That's what I'll probably do."

The conversation had an ominous ring in Cameron's ears. He had the feeling, amounting to a near certainty, that Madeleine wouldn't take kindly to his decision of yesterday. Retiring here to the Highlands just would not commend itself to her. An Englishwoman, Madeleine instinctively preferred to move south rather than north. Cameron himself had spent his youth in the north, but had been educated later, both at school and university, in England. He had no accent in speech, but he retained the fluency in Gaelic which he acquired in his earliest years through playing with lads from the crofts south of Glenelg. He had spent both school holidays and university holidays in the far northwest, maintaining the ancient language with a fervent determination, since it was only through the language that he could link himself with the past tradition of the Highland people.

The weather was no better the following day, so immediately after breakfast Cameron telephoned through to the National Radioastronomy Observatory near Pitlochry. He was able to fix an appointment to see Dr. Fielding "at some time in the early afternoon." He and Madeleine were away by 9 A.M. Driving once more along Glen Shiel, Cameron glanced up to the right in the direction of the Saddle. Heavy clouds were swirling about the summit. He caught a glimpse of snow on the upper slopes of Faochag. They hit a squall of rain a few miles beyond Cluanie. It hammered furiously on the windshield. The car bumped and made crablike movements as the powerful gusts caught it from the western side. Not a day to be out on the tops.

Beyond Cluanie they took the Invermoriston road. Madeleine would have preferred to swing south to Invergarry. She had been hoping the call back to London would stop her husband from visiting Strathfarrar. He said he only wanted to make inquiries about Pancho, but she suspected the so-called inquiries would soon turn into a violent and flaming quarrel.

Sure enough, Cameron swung left off the Inverness road at Drumnadrochit. Half an hour later they were through Cannich. At Struy they turned left into a narrow but well-paved road. Three hundred yards along it, the way was barred by a heavy wooden gate. With a grunt, Cameron was out of the car. His head down against the wind, he made over to a whitewashed stone lodge on the left. Madeleine saw him talking and gesticulating to an elderly woman. Then he came back and studied the gate. It was heavily chained with as many as ten different padlocks along the chain. He also studied the hinges and then got back into the car. In silence he reversed the car, drove back to the main road and turned left for Inverness.

"She's had orders to let no one through," he said by way of explanation.

"Why?"

"Stalking."

"But we're not intending going out on the hills."

"Yes, but she wasn't to know that. I couldnt press too much. She must do what she's told to do, poor devil."

"Why are we going this way?"

"So that I can try for a key at the Lovatt office in Beauly."

"We're going to be late. It's half past ten already."

"We'll get onto the A9 south. It's faster than going down the Great Glen."

"I suppose so. What was the reason for the extraordinary number of padlocks on the gate?"

"Each landlord has his own. They can't trust each other, apparently. I found out the name of the man who shot Pancho We'll soon track him down."

About one-third of the way through Beauly they stopped ou side a stone house.

"I seem to remember this is the Lovatt place," mutter Cameron. He went inside and immediately found a girl rattli away on a typewriter.

27

"Is this the Lovatt office?"

"It is."

"I wish to inquire about a key to the road up Strathfarrar."

"Oh."

Cameron guessed from the monosyllable, and from the cloud which flitted across the girl's face, that he was in for trouble. She led him to an office on the first floor. Opening the door, she said to a small man seated at a desk covered with papers:

"There's a gentleman here asking for a key to Strathfarrar."

"Can't be done."

"And why would that be?" asked Cameron, pushing past the girl.

"No keys during the stalking season."

This was accompanied by a wave of the hand, to indicate that the subject was closed.

"Look, my name is Cameron."

"I'm happy to meet you, Mr. Cameron, but there is nothing I can do for you."

"A dog of mine was shot in Strathfarrar. About two weeks ago. I want to make inquiries about it from one of the local farmers."

"Ah!"

Another monosyllable and another cloud. This time the cloud settled, rather than flitted, on the man's face.

"It is preposterous," went on Cameron, "that my dog should be shot and that I should be prevented from talking to the man who did it."

"There is nothing to stop you from walking."

"There is nothing to stop me from banging your head against the wall, little man."

Cameron saw from the blank expression that the Gaelic wasn't understood, which was perhaps just as well.

"Look, Mr. Cameron, let me presume to give you a bit of advice," said the fellow, getting up from his desk. "Keep away

from Strathfarrar. If your dog was the one I think it was—a big white brute—you won't find yourself popular in Strathfarrar. Or in a lot of other places."

The dialogue was ended by the arrival of a gray-haired man of about sixty, dressed in Highland fashion, kilt, sporran, dirk in stocking.

"Morning, Macintosh," he said, walking into the office and addressing the little man, just as if Cameron were not there.

"Morning, Sir William."

"I'll not be doubting you have a padlock of your own."

Sir William apparently did not understand the Gaelic either. Cameron felt an icy rage. With commanding deliberation, he studied the man's attire, from bonnet down to the trim brown shoes.

"A farce is this?" he asked explosively.

But neither Macintosh nor Sir William understood. Even if they had understood the language, it is doubtful that they would have understood Cameron's meaning.

Madeleine could see from her husband's face that he had drawn another blank, which did not displease her.

"There are times when the police are useful and important, and there are times when the police are an unmitigated nuisance," muttered Cameron as he turned the car once again and headed south.

"By which I suppose you mean you would have enjoyed beating some unfortunate person to a jelly."

"By which I mean that some issues cannot be resolved by modern polite conventions."

They reached Inverness, ignoring the eastern by-pass. It took only a few moments to negotiate the bridge across the Ness, to turn up the hill past the red-stone imitation castle, and to negotiate the oddly suburban lanes with which the A9 starts south of the town.

Cameron had no thought of quitting the main road. Indeed

Madeleine could see it was his intention to drive straight through to Pitlochry and she was wondering just where she could persuade him to stop for lunch. Yet some three to four miles south of Inverness Cameron turned away left. The sign to Culloden Moor caught his eye. On an instant impulse he decided to visit the Jacobite battlefield.

He had been there twice before, the first time as a boy of twelve. Old Hector, who worked for his father, had taken him. Hector MacDonald had been a Lovatt Scout in the Boer War. Often enough he would talk to the youthful Cameron of his experiences in South Africa. And often enough the talk would swing around to the old battle of Culloden. Old Hector knew the details. He knew the order of the clans. He was at pains to explain why the MacDonalds were positioned away on the left. He knew where Keppoch had died. Young Cameron had stood in awe at the Bloody Wall. Then he had charged himself across the selfsame ground where the clan Cameron, with Murray's men close on the right, had breached the English line. His cries had rung out on the afternoon air as he imagined himself in hand-to-hand combat with Barrel's regiment.

The second visit came ten years later. By this time Cameron was a university graduate. He came to Culloden with an American named MacGillivray. This second visit had been one of sadness. Sadness for the unnecessary suffering. Sadness for the persecution which forced so many Highlanders to leave their homes to become scattered throughout the world. Sadness that brutality was so much a normal feature of the human animal.

This third visit, on a windy October day, turned out differently again. It came as an intense shock to find the battlefield grown over by woodland. Cameron parked the car some two hundred yards back from the memorial cairn. Leaving Madeleine there, he walked to the clan graves. At least the graves had been left in open ground. He stood for a while. Then, as he walked away toward the trees, a black fury seized him. This was the final indignity. Not content with cruelty and persecution, not content with stealing the land, not content with evictions, not content with an endless draining of vigor from the Highlands, they must even obliterate the very ground on which men had fought and died. Obliterated by mean trees, not even dignified trees of good quality. Obliterated by the very poorest quality trees. What was it but a part of a determined degradation of the old culture by these unremitting creatures to the south?

"May the wrath of God strike you sometime," Cameron muttered.

A girl had come cycling along the road. She dismounted near the clan graves, left her machine at the edge of the road, and walked over the grass to one of the stones. Cameron didn't notice her until she was already returning to the road. Then he saw a single rose in front of the stone marking the Stewarts of Appin.

"You brought the flower?"

He thought the girl was about twelve, about the same age he had been when first he had come to the Moor with old Hector. So many years ago now.

"Yes, sir."

"Why?"

"I come every week, for my mother."

"The Stewarts of Appin, they were your people?"

The girl nodded.

"Are you English, sir?" she asked.

"No; why would I be English?"

"The way you talk, sir."

Cameron smiled and pointed toward the line of attack across the battlefield.

"My ancestor was out there. We stood to the right of your people."

31

"Who would that be, sir?"

"Lochiel."

The girl's dark eyes widened in astonishment. Then a look of disbelief flashed across the young face.

"Away with you now. Tell your mother that in a time she should send a flower for the Cameron."

The girl jumped to her cycle, in a hurry to be away, as if she was at last aware that she had been talking to a ghost.

"Wait until the spring, and then bring the flower," Cameron called after her.

He made his way slowly back to the car. It was not until they were again on the A9 that Madeleine asked, "Did you talk with the girl on a bicycle?"

"Yes; why?"

"She was crying as she passed by."

4

The Radiotelescope

They drove south through Carrbridge and Kingussie to Dalwhinnie, where they stopped for lunch. There was little traffic on this wild October day, so after lunch they were soon over the pass to Blair Atholl and thence to Pitlochry, where they took the branch road east toward Kirkmichael. Some fifteen miles along this road, near Straloch, they turned north onto a still smaller road, which led, after winding at first through fields and then through barren low hills, at last to the Observatory. Already, three miles away, they could see the great 450-foot dish silhouetted starkly against the wintry sky. In spite of its forbidding aspect, the site was well chosen. With the Grampians rising away to the north, it was not a region which welcomed "development." Except for an occasional passing aircraft, the Observatory was free from manmade electrical disturbances. Yet it was not more than twenty-five miles from the main-line railway station at Pitlochry.

Fielding was waiting for them. Cameron had met Fielding once or twice before and knew him as an overwhelming enthusiast. After introducing Madeleine, Cameron hinted, very broadly indeed, that she would prefer to spend the next hour or so drinking a quiet cup of tea in front of a fire, reading the morning paper, rather than be shown the wonders of the world's greatest radiotelescope. As for himself, he would be delighted to see the wonders of the world's greatest radiotelescope, even in the teeth of the gale now raging from the southwest. Fielding found this statement impossible to misinterpret, so he took them to his house—a finely converted stone farmstead—introduced Madeleine to his housekeeper and then swept Cameron, without ceremony, back to the radiotelescope.

Fielding was a big man. The vast horn-rimmed glasses which he sported gave him a permanently sleepy look. This he had turned to great advantage throughout his career. In point of fact, not a glance, not a whisper escaped him. Gifted with both shrewdness and tact, when he needed them, he was adapted naturally for a career of the greatest distinction in politics. Yet politics interested him not at all, except in one respect. Freakishly, he was consumed with an abiding passion for astronomy, and it was in regard to the interests of astronomy that he displayed his political gifts. The great telescope which Cameron now gazed up at, admittedly in some awe, was decisive evidence of Fielding's political skills. The only reason why he hadn't terrified Whitehall into providing him with funds for a still larger instrument was because he didn't know how to build one. This was the largest size that his driving energy had yet been able to bring to fruition.

Cameron was well used to scientific instruments of great size, but on the ground, stretching over large horizontal distances. This telescope, with its many thousands of tons of steel, was up in the air towering above his head. These astronomers had determination even to conceive of a thing like this, let alone build it. Fielding insisted on taking him up there into the vast parabolic bowl. It was like being in a new world, an abstract world of metal arranged in precise geometrical shapes. The rim of the bowl reared above them so they were not conscious at all of the outside world. The eye adjusted its scale in a curious way, so that it all seemed incredibly vast. Cameron had the impression of a "whiteout" on a great snowfield.

The evening light was already fading and the aircraft warning lights on the bowl were switched on by the time Fielding had completed his tour of the actual telescope. Now he was all agog to show Cameron the intricacies of the electronic drive and control. To Fielding the electronics were the main marvel of the Observatory. But nuclear physics is well ahead of astronomy in its development of electronics, so there was nothing here to cause Cameron even to lift his eyebrows. This part of the installation seemed very straightforward.

Yet Fielding had held the best for last. On a table in a well-lit office were spread rolls of paper. He smoothed out one of them and pointed at a wavy ink line which ran along the roll.

"Think there's anything here, Cameron?"

It was an ordinary pen recorder. The trace was mostly irregular, of the kind which physicists describe as "noise." But at the place where Fielding was pointing the trace rose higher.

"This is a sweep across one of the gas clouds in the plane of the galaxy."

"Along the chart?"

"Yes."

"What does the output represent?"

"The difference between the signal and a fixed load."

"I see."

"Well, what's the verdict?"

To Cameron the signal was fairly obvious, but then you never could be sure of anything with astronomers—they did things in a peculiar way. "I don't know enough about the setup to offer an opinion," he answered.

"Cautious, eh. Well, take a look at this." Fielding pointed at another roll. "We've got something different here. The dish is pointing all the time at the cloud."

"Tracking on it?"

"Right. And we're doing a frequency switch now, backward and forward through a resonant frequency."

"You mean its line emission?"

"Right. Wavelength a bit above five cm."

"Of what?"

"Ah ha! That's the question, isn't it?" Fielding grinned.

"I suppose it is."

Fielding thumped the table in excitement. His eyes shone. "Glycine," he roared. Then he pointed at a blackboard, at a chemical symbol:

$$H_2N-CH_2-\overset{\displaystyle O}{\overset{|}{C}}-OH$$

Noticing the tell tale CO—OH group, Cameron asked, "Amino acid?"

"Right. First detection of an amino acid."

"This is getting pretty complicated. How far d'you think it's possible to go? I mean up to what size of molecule?"

"So far as the gas itself is concerned I doubt if there's a limit."

"Up to macromolecules?"

"Right—if we can find 'em. But it's like looking for a needle in a haystack."

"How's that?"

"Well, you can't do this sort of thing unless you know just what to look for. Complicated molecules have a vast number of possible frequencies. The trouble is to find 'em. In the lab, I mean. To sort 'em out properly. Take glycine. To begin with, you even have trouble in the lab getting amino acids out of solution—into the gas phase."

"But you managed it."

"Not here, of course. You need a full-scale chemical lab. This rotational frequency for glycine was found at Imperial College."

"You couldn't find it astronomically until you knew where to look?"

"Right. That's where this microwave spectroscopy is different from optical spectroscopy. We have to know what to look for first. The optical guys just take a spectrum and then sort it out afterwards."

Cameron could see that Fielding was as pleased as a dog with two tails. And in a general way—a non-astronomer's way —Cameron could see that he had a right to be so. Amino acids are the building blocks for proteins. Proteins, suitably organized, become life. Was there life everywhere throughout the vast interstellar spaces? It was certainly beginning to look that way. He asked about it as they drove from the telescope back to Fielding's home.

"Well, that's a bit ambitious, isn't it?" answered Fielding. "It goes a long way beyond anything we know at present."

This was the first time Cameron had heard an astronomer expressing a cautious view.

It had been Cameron's intention to leave in the early evening, but Fielding would have none of it. He insisted that Cameron and Madeleine should spend the night there, since in truth it was rare that he had a visitor of Cameron's distinction. Besides, he wanted to talk at some length about the Australian venture. So after an excellent supper prepared by his housekeeper, he ushered Cameron into his study for a glass of port, leaving Madeleine to read or talk to the housekeeper—which dismissal she was well used to, being a "science wife." Cameron managed to swap the port for whisky. Unlike his host, he had no taste for sweet stuff.

"I'd say you've bought a can of worms," Fielding began with an air of well-being and satisfaction. He sipped his port and toasted slippered feet in front of an open fire.

"How's that?"

"What you're going to find is that the British have plenty of good reasons why the Australian ideas are wrong, and the Australians will have plenty of good arguments why the British proposal is wrong. As sure as God made little apples, that's what you're going to find."

"I've found it already."

"Good. Then all you need to know is that both are right and both are wrong. Right when they object to the other fellow. Wrong when they make proposals themselves."

"You mean it isn't possible to make a dish either way."

"Not at their wavelengths, from 3 cm down to 0.8 mm. Tunable surfaces are too fiddling and deformable surfaces too unstable. In a way this makes your job easy. Just say both sides are wrong."

Fielding put a large hunk of wood on the fire, took up his glass again and went on. "Besides, the wavelength range isn't right. Much better to go much shorter. If it was my project I'd go down to 0.2 mm, at least."

"Wouldn't that make things worse?"

"No, because I'd be satisfied with a much smaller dish, something like fifty feet. You see, there are many more lines to work on at the shorter wavelengths. It's a much richer field."

"But the one you showed me this afternoon was long wavelength."

"Right, above five cm. The way it goes is this: At the long waves there aren't too many possibilities, but for what there are—well, you can go to work on 'em with a big telescope. So you can get to grips with very sensitive cases, like glycine. At the short wavelengths it's the opposite way. There are lots of possibilities but you can't have the sensitivity of a really big dish."

Cameron took a sharp gulp of whisky. As it warmed its way downward from his throat he nodded, and then grunted, "So it's a case of trying to have the best of both worlds. This project I'm supposed to be looking into?"

"You've got it in a nutshell—trying to have the best of both worlds—going shorter in wavelength but still trying for a big dish. It won't work. They'll end up by falling between two stools. I've told 'em so, but my views weren't popular."

"I'd have thought your views would carry a lot of weight."

"No, because I'm supposed to have a conflict of interest. There are plenty of people to argue that until this new telescope is built we're top dog—here. The argument is that once . . ."

". . . the new telescope is built you won't be top dog."

"Right. At any rate in their kind of work. There'll still be lots of other work for us to do at the longer wavelengths."

"Do you have a conflict of interest?"

"Maybe. It's always hard to judge your own inner feelings. And it's also hard to judge objectively how far new manufacturing techniques might just make this thing possible. That'll be for you to decide—not me, thank god."

"You suggested just now a smaller dish at still shorter wavelengths."

"Ah, yes. I'd be interested in that myself. If I hadn't so much on my plate already."

"You'd do what?"

"Go round to the biggest people in the capital goods industry. Vickers here in this country, Krupps in Germany, Japan Steel or Mitsubishi, several firms in the U.S. Find out who has the biggest lathe and get them to turn out the biggest feasible precision dish. I'd take the best I could get. It's a brand-new field and nobody else can be doing any better. The thing would be to move quickly. Get some zip into it. Stop all the argument and the political nonsense."

"Why aren't they doing just that?"

"Because the receivers are tricky at these very short wavelengths. There's a reluctance to jump into unfamiliar electronics. But with your backup from CERN this shouldn't frighten you."

"No, but I don't want to get actively involved."

"I can understand that, assuming the 1000-Gev is on. Is it, by the way?"

"Still in the negotiation stages. We're hoping it's going ahead. If it does I won't have any time for millimeter telescopes."

Fielding nodded, and then nodded again, and almost imperceptibly again. Cameron waited for a moment but there was no response. He looked curiously at the other man and realized that he had fallen asleep. Gone out like pressing a switch. Incredulously, he watched as Fielding's breathing became gradually deeper and deeper. Then he tiptoed from the room to find Madeleine preparing for bed.

The following morning they learned from the housekeeper that Fielding had stayed up very late—working—and that "the Doctor" would not be joining them for breakfast. Cameron wondered if Fielding had just gone on and on sleeping in front of the fire until at last he awoke stiff as a board. As they drove away south, down the mountain road toward Pitlochry, he doubted if they would ever find out. They parted company at Pitlochry, Cameron to take the train for London and Madeleine to return with the car to Glen Shiel. They made arrangements for meeting three weeks hence in Geneva. Madeleine waved as the train rumbled out of the station, the scarf about her throat flying in the wind.

In spite of recent improvements, the bad stretch of road from Pitlochry to Blair Atholl still needed care, so it was not until north of Clachan that Madeleine could turn her mind to a problem which had been causing her to worry in a long-drawn-out kind of way. The unrest in her husband's mind had been growing now for some time. It was almost at a point where it must be noticed by other people. She thought it was a combination of three things. Age, of course. At fifty a man should be easing off. Instead the load was growing heavier. Twenty years ago, even ten years ago, the strain had been largely scientific. It had been a case of doing the right thing scientifically, simply of being on top of the work itself. Now there was a big political job, an external relations job, as well. Assessing projects, like this thing in Australia, talking to politicians and that sort of thing. Even persuading scientists not to quarrel among themselves. How to prevent the pushy ones from outweighing the shyer competent ones. The normal thing to do to ease all this pressure would be to slacken off, particularly on the laboratory side. But her husband wouldn't hear of that. Cameron insisted everything else would then become meaningless. Madeleine couldn't quite see why it should. Most other scientists went that way, and they seemed happy enough. Madeleine drove on, a dark frown across her face. She had suspected for some time now that he was planning to push ahead to some position, to some conclusion, and then to ditch everything. She more than suspected it was his intention to retire up here to the Highlands. She glanced out of the car, at the wastes of the Drumochter Pass, and shuddered.

Cameron reached London in the late afternoon. He again made his way to the Royal Society in Carlton House Terrace. Here he put through a long telephone call to Geneva. Then he called Henry Mallinson, who instantly suggested they should dine together at the Athenaeum Club. Cameron would have preferred a different style and standard of food, but agreed to the Athenaeum since it would be easier to talk quietly there than in a crowded restaurant.

Mallinson appeared sharply at 6:45 P.M. They had a quick drink and then went immediately into the dining room. It was very nearly empty, quite different from lunchtime, when it was full chock-a-block with Whitehall types. A thought flashed through Cameron's mind: someone had once said that nothing would do more to put Britain on its feet again than total disaster to the Athenaeum at 1:45 P.M. He tried to remember who it was and thought it might be J. B. Priestley. He was tempted to ask Mallinson but wisely desisted.

A waitress brought them a thin soup. As Cameron looked it over with a baleful eye, Mallinson said, "They've appointed their arbitrator."

"My opponent?"

41

"Oh, I wouldn't look at it that way."

"You wouldn't?"

"No, not at all. There's been enough disagreement on this project already."

"Who would my opponent be?"

"Oh, well, if you're in a mood—one of your Celtic moods —your colleague is Nygaard."

"Danish?" asked Cameron in some surprise.

"No, no. Bob Nygaard. National Radioastronomy Observatory, Charlottesville, Virginia. American."

"Ah ha! I see."

"You see what?"

"Why you're in such high spirits, Henry."

"I wasn't aware . . ."

"Oh, yes, you are. High spirits, excellent spirits. After all, with me British and Nygaard American, and therefore neutral, it should be an easy victory for our side, shouldn't it?"

"If I may say so, that would be just the wrong way to look at it."

"But that's the way you'd like it to come out?"

"I wouldn't be human if I didn't hope that our chaps will come out in the end to have been right. But the really important thing is for you to convince *both* sides. Let me make this clear. You will have failed, whatever you decide, unless you carry *both* sides with you."

"So the real thing is harmony. Sweet harmony—eh, Henry?"

"Don't let that mood carry you too far," muttered Mallinson.

He shoveled a spoonful of cabbage in the last stages of watery disintegration onto his plate. Cameron marveled at the relish with which he did so.

"Hasn't it occurred to you, Henry, that it might have been as well for our side to have sought a neutral opinion. Someone from the German place at Bonn, shall we say?"

"I regard you as neutral, my dear Cameron. After all, you've been out of the country for quite a number of years. Incidentally, when are you CERN people going to recommend an international facility in this country?"

"First, when the Treasury agree to reasonable tax arrangements. Second, when the British stop cooking cabbage like that," Cameron pointed rudely at his companion's plate.

Mallinson grimaced. "I understand exactly what you mean. I eat it as a sort of self-discipline. Like yoga."

"Does your wife still practice it?"

"What, yoga or the cabbage?"

"Yoga."

"She has spells of it, on and off. Mostly off, these days, thank god."

"Must be very disconcerting, the staring out into space."

"Especially after a long day at the office."

"But seriously, wouldn't it be better for you to ask someone from Bonn? In the first place it would be tactful—and in the second place they know much more about this thing than I do."

Mallinson sighed. "I know. But our radioastronomers just wouldn't accept it. They'll accept you."

"But the Australians have accepted Nygaard."

"Which is their affair, isn't it?"

Cameron bit into a piece of Bakewell tart. "Puts me in an awkward spot, though."

"You're used to it. To worse."

"At least there's some advantage in not having to go to Australia. Virginia isn't so bad."

"Oh, but you must go to Australia."

"Why?"

"To talk to the Australians. So they'll feel they're getting a fair crack of the whip."

"Look, Henry, let us use a little common sense. I have a crowded schedule—"

"Excuse me, but in my office the other day you were complaining—complaining loudly—of *delay*."

"Which doesn't mean that I don't—"

"On this I am adamant, my dear fellow. You *must* go to Australia. Both you and Nygaard *must* go to Australia."

Cameron shrugged as he got to his feet at the end of the meal. The two men walked over to a desk by the door, where they paid their respective bills. Then they strode up a broad flight of stairs to an upstairs lounge. Cameron poured the coffee. "Black, isn't it?"

"Thank you. No sugar."

As they relaxed in large chairs, Mallinson lit a cigar, sipped his coffee and said, "My spies tell me you dropped in to see Fielding."

"I hadn't met him before."

"You found him interesting."

"Yes. He's got an interesting place up there."

Mallinson nodded. "Perhaps I should strike a warning note."

"About what?"

"Fielding."

"Don't tell me, Henry. I know all about it already."

"What!"

"At night he falls asleep in front of the fire," said Cameron.

"It was hardly his sleeping habits that I had in mind. What I wanted to tell you is that Fielding is believed to be planning a new instrument."

"Oh?"

"Yes, for the wavelength range from 3 cm down to 0.8 mm."

Cameron gulped the rest of his coffee, stared for a moment at Mallinson, thought for a few seconds and half smiled in the direction of two men at a neighboring table. Both were in black, both clergymen. One was clearly a bishop. Cameron found himself trying to decide the style of the other man.

5

Journey to Australia

Cameron caught the noon plane the following day from London
to Washington. To his relief it was one of the older planes,
not a Jumbo. It landed at Dulles, which meant he had to take
a taxi the thirty miles or so to the City Airport, where he was
just in time to make the connection for Charlottesville. The
small Piedmont plane bucketed a good deal when it reached
the Blue Ridge, which wasn't so good following the eight-hour
crossing of the Atlantic. Nygaard was waiting at the exit gate.

"Dr. Cameron? Yes? Bob Nygaard."

"Glad to meet you. We've got a bit of a problem on our
hands."

"Sure have. 'Did you have a good trip?' to quote Chief Justice Warren."

"How's that?"

"The opening remark of the Warren Commission: 'Did you
have a good trip here, Mrs. Oswald?' Set the tone for the whole
thing. You've got bags?"

"Two."

"O.K. The baggage claim is just around here to the left."

As the plane had been a small one, the bags appeared in
good time. Taking one each, the two men were soon away in
Nygaard's car.

"I haven't arranged anything for this evening. I didn't think you'd be feeling like any social engagements. But you're welcome to come around to my house for a drink and dinner."

"To be frank, I'm feeling like a very light meal and then immediately to bed," answered Cameron.

"I thought you might be. We've booked you into the Country Inn. It's not too near the Observatory, but it's comfortable."

"Sounds fine."

"I'll be in the office first thing in the morning, and I'll be available all day."

"Not like Japan," said Cameron, stating the obvious.

"Japan?"

"We had some steel work done in Japan. Their engineers met me at the airport, straight out from Switzerland, without any stopover. Straight to the office for a business meeting. Keen fellows."

"Shucks, we won't work you that hard."

Cameron was soon in bed, but although he was tired, sleep didn't come easily. He decided his heartbeat was too fast. The vibration of the plane somehow disturbed the body juices, damn it. Then he slept uneasily for a couple of hours, took two aspirins and slept again until about 3 A.M., which would be breakfast time back in Europe. He switched on the light over the bed and read through a file of papers. About an hour later, grunting and cursing, he switched off the light, and somehow managed to doze until six-thirty. He got up and shaved, took another shower and dressed in a leisurely way. By now the coffee shop should be open for breakfast. Oddly enough, he felt quite well.

The coffee shop was in fact just on the point of opening. He ordered orange juice, hot cakes and coffee, and then went off to buy a newspaper. The hot cakes were the best thing he'd eaten since the dinner at Fielding's house. Cameron decided that America led the world on two culinary items, prime ribs and hot cakes. He felt this thought justified a second helping and then sternly suppressed any such notion. When he paid his check the girl at the cash register was inclined to be chatty, so he asked her why they didn't serve porridge.

Cameron spent the next hour making a call to Geneva, just in case there was something new on the 1000-Gev front. There wasn't. He found himself wondering whether in this case no news was really good news. Then he ordered a taxi. A half hour's ride brought him to the Observatory building. Nygaard had been as good as his word. He was there, already at work, even though the clock in the corridor read only 8:30.

"Ah, good morning. I hope you slept well."

"As well as could be expected."

"I know what you mean. Look, Dr. Cameron, let me begin with a sort of apology."

"Over what?"

"Well, naturally I'd hoped to go with you to Australia, but this week happens to be bad for me. Our board has a meeting here on Friday."

"You can't come?"

"Not until after Friday. I'd like to go right away . . ."

"Obviously you can't. Anyway, you're advising on this business out of the kindness of your heart."

"I'm glad you see it that way. I could start out Saturday, but even Saturday would be awkward. You see, there's always a lot to be done. . . ."

"When can you start—Monday?"

"Yes, I could manage Monday."

"Then I'll simply spend a few days en route. I don't see there's much point in me getting there ahead of you."

"Well, shall we get down to the nitty-gritty?" Nygaard picked up a fistful of papers. "How are you getting on with this stuff?"

"I've made some kind of a shot at it. I've asked my chaps in

Geneva to check up and to extend some of the calculations."

"Could I ask how you came into it? Is CERN involved?"

"No, CERN isn't involved. Our science ministry consulted me."

"I see. I asked because of the European Southern Observatory. That's been referred to CERN, hasn't it?"

"Not my department," said Cameron, "but as it happens we've a fair amount of expertise on the structural side. So I've asked for computer programs to be run. The point which hits you in the eye when you read the deformable structure section —the Australian part, I mean—is that while they've worked out the normal modes of the antenna itself there's no guarantee at all that the modes are really stable."

"When there's an external power source?"

"Either in the drive motors, or just the wind."

"So you've doubts about the Australian position?"

Cameron nodded and Nygaard went on, "Fair enough. But do you really see the British proposal? Your people want to make up a dish out of more than a hundred separate petals. Can you see yourself tuning 'em all to an accuracy of better than a millimeter?"

"No." Cameron shook his head.

"Then where are we?"

"We're fine, because we're not making this damn telescope. My view, admittedly only an outsider's first impression, is that *both* proposals are suspect."

"Have you heard about the last National Academy report on astronomy?"

"No."

"Well, about two years ago the National Academy formed a committee to order priorities in U.S. astronomy. The idea was to stop competing projects from canceling each other out."

"When it came to funding?"

"Right. Well, the committee's first idea was to recommend

a dish of about this size for about this wavelength range. And they started by giving it top priority." Once again Nygaard brandished the papers.

"Then they got around to thinking about how they'd build it, which was where the trouble started. I know because I was on the committee myself. We decided in the end the thing was so difficult we just couldn't keep top priority for it. So we moved other projects ahead of it. So I guess I'm agreeing with you. Except that we're not at all certain that an automatically deformable dish couldn't be made. It'll be hard but maybe they can do it."

A secretary came in. "Would you like coffee?"

"Ah, Nona, this is Dr. Cameron."

Cameron shook hands with the girl.

"How d'you like it, Dr. Cameron?"

"With a little cream and no sugar."

The coffee came quickly and Cameron began sipping it as Nygaard repeated, "Maybe they can do it . . . maybe."

"Would you see us recommending something much smaller but at a higher frequency, say a forty-foot dish to operate down to two mm?"

Nygaard pursed his lips, tapped the desk and looked out into space for a moment. Then he stared unblinkingly at Cameron. "I think I'd better declare an interest on that one. A forty-foot telescope operating at two mm in Australia would put our own thirty-six-foot at Kitt Peak right out of business."

"Which puts you in an awkward spot?"

"Not really. I was asked to express an opinion on the respective merits of these two proposals." Nygaard brought his fist down on the papers. "Which isn't the same thing as open-ended advice."

Cameron finished the coffee. He felt he was beginning to see his way through this business. In fact half his mind was already occupied with the problem of how he was going to spend the next week. Should it be Berkeley? Hawaii or Tahiti? Or the Blue Ridge?

"How are the fall colors right now?" he asked.

Nygaard's eyes widened in surprise at this sudden change of subject. "Well, of course they're at their best right now. But . . ."

"I was thinking I might go up to the Blue Ridge."

"We can let you have one of our cars."

"I'd thought of walking. Isn't there a trail?"

"A hundred miles of it. I walked the whole length of it three years ago. Take a car to one of the best bits and start walking from there. When you're through walking just call us and we'll arrange to have you picked up."

Cameron had never ceased to marvel at the adaptability of Americans. Nygaard had permitted the subject to be switched without seeming out of countenance in the smallest degree. Yet he was curious.

"But how . . ." he began.

"How are we going to report?" answered Cameron. "Very simply, like this: Subject to our calculations and perhaps subject to what we find on the spot in Australia, we are going to report that both these proposals appear impracticable to us. You will leave it at that, because for you to say anything more would be an embarrassment. I shall probably suggest that it would be worthwhile considering a much smaller dish at higher frequency."

Nygaard was tapping the desk again. "It might change my point of view if there were a possibility of us joining in on a two-mm dish. Congress is strong on international projects right now. Would it seem improper to you if I were to fly a kite in that direction?"

Cameron laughed. "The project I run at CERN involves ten different countries. So I'm hardly the man to object to multinational activities. Anyway, my job is to make the best recommendation I can. It stops there."

"We do have quite a bit of expertise on front ends," Nygaard added reflectively.

Cameron thought for a moment of requesting information on front ends and then desisted. He found himself wondering if he would be able to buy a pair of comfortable walking boots here in Charlottesville.

Cameron liked to feel he had made correct decisions. It pleased him as he walked the Blue Ridge to feel that he'd done the right thing. He knew it was right because last night he'd slept a full ten hours without waking, which was rare these days. This was after spending two days in Charlottesville, buying the things he needed, talking to the scientists there, and socializing. Then he'd driven the hundred miles or so from Charlottesville and taken off into the woods. Nygaard was right when he said the fall colors would be magnificent. The brilliant and blazing reds of the forest in their full intensity was a sight that a European could hardly imagine.

Cameron was now in his third day away from the car. The trail was unpaved, except when it passed an occasional inn or motel. It simply led along through the trees, with views in great shafts to the east and west. Cameron guessed it to be Indian in the first place. There was a kind of delicacy about it—it went neatly around obstacles instead of smashing its way through them.

It was easy to imagine oneself out of the twentieth century, back to the times of the early settlers. Of all places in the United States it is perhaps easiest to turn time backward here in Virginia. Cameron's mind flicked to the battlefield of Culloden, 1746. The same brutish fools who had suppressed and desecrated the Scottish Highlands had lost the American colonies only thirty years later. Looking back over what Britain had managed to throw away in two centuries of stupidity and misrule, Cameron was convinced that verily this was a nation with a death wish.

51

So why was he troubling himself with this silly business of the radiotelescope? A squirrel crossed his path. He kicked a small stone in its direction and the creature leaped in a flash to the upper branches of a neighboring tree. Why indeed? At least he had been glad to find that Fielding's advice seemed good to Nygaard, in fact too good for Nygaard's peace of mind. Cameron had put Fielding down as an honest scientist and consequently had been inclined to discount Mallinson's warning. He was glad to find his judgment confirmed. Cameron knew all about empire-building scientists. He had seen plenty of national physics programs ruined by such people. This was why he preferred working at an international laboratory. With many nations involved there was less room for the scientific prima donna. Less room for chaps, equipped by nature with elephant hides, who spend their lives trumpeting their own causes on parochial national committees. Cameron wondered how long things would stay relatively clean even at the international level. He decided he was getting grumpy, which meant he ought to be thinking about lunch. Consulting his map, he saw there was a likely-looking place about four miles ahead. With a determined swing he stepped up his pace. If he kept to it, he would be there within the hour.

It was with regret that after two further days on the Blue Ridge, Cameron at last put through a call to Charlottesville. He did this on Sunday evening, the day before Nygaard would be ready to leave for Australia. He made arrangements for a car to be sent for him the following morning.

Reaching Charlottesville again by midday Monday, this left two hours before Cameron and Nygaard were to catch a plane for Roanoke and New Orleans. From New Orleans there was a direct afternoon flight to San Francisco. The QANTAS plane from San Francisco to Sydney left at 9 P.M.

With stops in Hawaii and Fiji, they reached Sydney about

7.30 A.M. the following morning. Allowing for summer time being still operative in California, and also for six hours' difference in longitude, the long flight across the Pacific had taken almost eighteen hours. From Charlottesville they had been traveling for more than twenty-hour hours, and Cameron was feeling decidedly creased. Even Nygaard, fifteen years younger, was now looking forward desperately to a shower and a few hours' sleep.

They were met by a reception party of considerable size, including a television crew. Cameron instantly vetoed any TV interview, whereupon a radioastronomer—whom Nygaard recognized and greeted—explained that it was the intention to take a further plane, leaving Sydney for Wombat Springs at 10:30 A.M. This meant the TV people in Sydney would not have the opportunity of interviewing them later in the day, or on the following day. Cameron said he understood the situation perfectly, and that the answer was still no.

When at last the Wombat Springs plane was ready for loading, Cameron sat himself firmly beside Nygaard. "Why are we going to this Wombat place?" he asked.

"They want to start by showing us where the telescope is to go."

"What if there's no telescope?"

"They haven't thought of that. All that's worrying them is the kind of telescope."

"Does it make a difference as to the site?"

"Not that I can see."

Cameron felt as if his head were coming off. If the site made no difference, why bother with it? But when the plane landed an hour later on a grassy upland field, his spirits lifted sharply at the sunlit beauty of the place.

The party and their bags were stowed into three large vehicles and they were away within minutes. A short drive took them into Wombat Springs. Cameron expected this little township to

53

be their destination, but the journey was still not at an end. They swung left off the wide main street and were quickly in open country again, now wilder than before. Cameron's spirits lifted further as he spotted several kangaroos grazing in a kind of rough parkland. He decided he would like to see a bit more of them, since these were his first wild ones. "Dr. Nygaard would like to take a look at the kangaroos," he yelled in his best battle-cry voice. The vehicles ground to a halt.

"Sure would," muttered Nygaard.

"Wallabies," said an Australian voice.

Nygaard began a long hunt in his bags, eventually emerging with his camera. Cameron, sensing that the party was somewhat bored, smiled benignly into the sunshine.

About ten miles from Wombat Springs they turned up the road to Mount Bogung. All along the steep roadside were plants like mimosa, which Cameron knew to be wattles, the subject of wattles being complex and subtle and dear to the hearts of most Australians. Anyway, Cameron thought the bright mimosa yellow looked well against the dark green of the trees. It would be hard to imagine a greater contrast between the green of these trees and the flaming leaves of the Blue Ridge forest. Yet each in its place looked right.

At the top of the mountain road the cars stopped. They all dismounted and walked two or three hundred yards across fairly flat ground to the site of the proposed radiotelescope. Cameron did his best to seem interested but his attention was mainly occupied by the mountains several miles away to the south, and by a number of spectacular steep cones of rock among them. He had the idea this might be the bowels of an ancient volcano, overgrown now by a profusion of plants and trees.

Then back to the cars and a final short ride along the mountaintop, past a vast white dome on the left and a smaller one on the right, to a building marked with the single word LODGE, where they were shown to separate rooms. Cameron found his to be surprisingly large and well appointed. Grudgingly, he admitted to himself he was glad after all that the party had not stayed in Sydney.

A young man, one of the car drivers, poked his head in at the door. "Lunch in ten minutes," he said and was gone. Cameron felt up to one final effort. He spent fifteen minutes unpacking and then went along a corridor toward a large common room. The others were already seated at a table well stocked with food. He decided to limit himself to soup and desert, a decision which the Australians—settling down to a good lunch—found hard to understand. Looking around the table, Cameron realized with a slight shock that although he'd been introduced to everyone there, he had not taken in a single name. Later, tomorrow, when he felt human again, he would have to depend on Nygaard, since the time for asking names was now past.

Cameron waited for the others to finish eating. Then he excused himself, returned to his room, finished unpacking, took a shower, and at last climbed into bed. Within seconds he was asleep.

6

Mount Bogung Observatory

Cameron woke twelve hours later, about 2 A.M. He ate some chocolate from a bar he always carried when he was traveling, and then fell asleep until 5 A.M. He ate more chocolate but sleep did not come again. So he decided to get up. The sun had just risen when he stepped outside into a brilliant morning. It took him half an hour to walk the mountaintop back to the spot where the radiotelescope was supposed to go. The rocks around the site looked rather splintered and he wondered about the quality of the foundations. Still, with enough care that should be a solvable problem. The effect of the traveling and the switch from night to day made him feel woozy, like a vague intoxication. He sat down and spent a long time gazing at the landscape to the south.

At length he wandered back along the flat ridge which formed the backbone of the mountain. Cameron had always supposed that astronomers chose their sites in desert country, so it surprised him to find the center of Australian astronomy in such a profusely wooded and rich place. He stopped by the big 150-inch dome. He peered into the windows of a long building, which he found to be a workshop. Small by the standards of nuclear physics. Then he made his way back to the lodge, where he found the housekeeper to be astir. She quickly provided him with a plate of bacon and eggs and a pot of hot coffee.

Cameron gathered from the housekeeper, Mrs. Hambly as she introduced herself, that the "astronomers" would not be "in" to breakfast. They were asleep, "poor things," after their night's work, from which Cameron deduced that the "astronomers" were those working on the optical telescopes. The radio-astronomers from Sydney would be "in" for breakfast, very definitely, if their scoffing of lunch the previous day was anything to go by.

Nygaard was next to appear, because he too was feeling the time shift. Cameron spent a few moments with him going over names and correlating them with appearances, as best he could remember appearances. Then Nygaard gave him the appalling news that the plan was to fly them all back to Sydney in the early afternoon, to be ready for a major conference at C.S.I.R.O. on the following day.

"Major conference be damned," grunted Cameron. He was on the point of adding that he preferred kangaroos to radio-astronomers when two of the unfortunate radioastronomers came in. Cameron placed them as Ken Wright and Doug Harrison. He hoped this was right because it was going to be embarrassing if it wasn't.

"I hear the intention is to return to Sydney today," began Cameron, not averse to locking horns immediately.

"That's right," said Harrison, pouring milk over his corn-flakes.

"Isn't there a plane from Wombat Springs to Sydney tomorrow morning?"

"Yes, but it wouldn't get us there in time for the start of the conference."

"Besides, you'll be wanting plenty of time to brush up on all those British arguments," added Wright with a grin.

Mount Bogung might be the site of an extinct volcano, but

Cameron could feel an active volcano boiling up inside himself. "Would the cause of science be seriously impeded if the conference should start a couple of hours later?" he asked with dangerous politeness.

"No, but the boss wouldn't like it," was Harrison's reply.

"I was just saying to Dr. Cameron that I'm not feeling too well," broke in Nygaard. "I'd be grateful if you'd put a call through to Sydney, saying that I'm really in need of a day's rest—to recover."

Cameron started to choke and stepped quickly outside. A moment later Nygaard joined him.

"What the devil did you say that for?" Cameron asked.

"Well, I'm their representative, aren't I?"

Cameron thought for an instant before nodding. "You'd make a good diplomat."

"You think so, huh?" Nygaard grinned. "Seriously though, it's a real paradox of America—the average citizen is reasonably courteous and diplomatic in a commonsense kind of way, yet our official diplomats are lousy."

"In the idiom of yesteryear, you can say that again."

"Look, I've got some stuff that's supposed to help with the time adjustment," went on Nygaard, "some kind of potassium salt. Supposed to help with the potassium ions in the blood. Whether it does I don't know, but you can try it if you like."

"Can't make things worse," commented Cameron gloomily.

Nygaard produced a bottle of small white pills, and Cameron gulped down four of them. He was just standing there wondering whether stuffing oneself full of potassium really did any good when Nygaard loosed off an enormous sneeze.

"I wasn't being altogether diplomatic," Nygaard muttered. "I've been feeling this coming on." Then he sneezed again and blew his nose determinedly in a fistful of paper tissues.

"It's the trip," grunted Cameron. "Changes the bodily equilibrium, which gives the bugs inside you a chance to get on top."

"Thanks for the opinion," said Nygaard through a forest of paper. "I'll be fine in a few hours. It's a sort of twenty-four-hour thing. I've had it happen before after a long flight. I keep wondering if it's psychosomatic," he muttered. Then he relapsed into a further sneezing bout.

Cameron went quickly back to the common room.

"There's no possibility of Dr. Nygaard traveling to Sydney today. He's come down with a virus, probably a twenty-four-hour attack," he informed the assembled radioastronomers. There were five of them, three others in addition to Ken Wright and Doug Harrison.

"Then we'll have to give that one away," said Harrison.

"We've been looking at the program for the conference," began one of the three whose names Cameron could not remember. "With a bit of rearranging we can keep the parts of concern to you and Dr. Nygaard out of the first morning's session."

"The idea was to talk about the telescope itself *before* coming to the problems we aim to tackle with it. But I suppose we could discuss the problems first," said another of the three.

"Which isn't a bad way to begin. That's the way I always begin myself," agreed Cameron.

"But we're reckoning that if a car meets your plane tomorrow morning we can have you at the lab by lunchtime. Then we can start discussing the structure in the afternoon."

"That's fine by me—assuming Dr. Nygaard isn't in a raging fever by then." Cameron saw they had telescope plans opened on the large table. "By the way," he went on, "I woke up in the night. There was a fairish wind blowing." From the ensuing silence he saw he'd touched on a sensitive point. "Won't the wind play merry hell with your nice deformable structure?"

"No worse than the British design," answered Ken Wright.

"Besides, the wind doesn't blow all the time," said one of the others.

"It blows often enough for the optical astronomers to have designed a very small slit for the dome of their big telescope. Why do you want to come here on the mountain at all? Why don't you keep down as low as possible?" asked Cameron.

"We need to come up as high as we can because of atmospheric absorption and because of phase distortions," explained Harrison.

At this point Mrs. Hambly asked for the table, which she wanted to begin setting for lunch. It was still only around noon, much earlier than lunchtime the previous day. This was to give the radioastronomers a meal before they had to leave for the Sydney plane. "There's no point in us staying. Besides we must be at the lab in time for the conference," said one of them. This made Cameron feel slightly guilty, which persuaded him the potassium really was doing him good. Mrs. Hambly brought in four vast bottles of beer. Yes, the fact that he enjoyed a glass of it was another point in favor of the potassium.

After lunch, Cameron waved the radioastronomers off in two of the big cars, feeling he must atone in some degree for his former surliness. Then he went to his room and tried to read a paper describing a new form of focusing for particles at very high energies. But his concentration was hopeless. So he consulted Mrs. Hambly about the possibility of someone driving him into the country to the south and west—the country he had looked out on during his early-morning walk. She soon discovered a young mechanic from the workshop who would be glad to do so. They took a smaller car, drove down the mountain road, and turned west in a direction opposite to Wombat Springs. Soon they were in country of a kind Cameron hadn't seen before, except very briefly and drowsily the previous day. It had the character of endlessly rolling parkland, dotted everywhere with little clumps of dark-green trees.

So anxious was the young lad to show Cameron whatever he wanted to see, and so many times did Cameron stop the car to examine a bush or a tree, to take a look at some new bird, or to climb a striking piece of rock, that dusk was falling on their return up the mountain road. There was only just time for a shower before dinner.

An entirely new set of faces occupied the common room. This was the night shift, working on the optical telescopes. One of them, a man a good half foot shorter than Cameron, came forward.

"John Almond."

The name was immediately familiar to Cameron. Almond was director of the Mount Bogung Observatory. He had the awkward job of dealing with both the Australian and British governments, the joint owners of the big 150-inch telescope. He also had a hundred and one different people and organizations trying to muscle in on the Observatory. Yet he contrived to run this endless obstacle course with apparent ease.

Cameron had often wondered how far a man's career in science depended on his appearance. A great deal, he had come to believe; or if not on appearance, at any rate on some arresting nonscientific quality. His own career had been markedly influenced by his height, six feet two inches. His distant forebears came to Scotland from Ireland, where, in the still more distant past, lived a people with the remarkable combination of light eyes and dark hair. According to some anthropologists this was a pre-Celtic people. Cameron's height, his light eyes and dark hair, instantly marked him out in a degree that was not given to men of undistinguished appearance.

So what of John Almond? Not much above five feet seven in height, without distinctive coloring, John Almond had no such advantages. But from his first words Cameron knew the quality which had lifted Almond to prominence, even in his youth. The voice, the deep voice of unusual timbre. Without real scientific ability the voice would not have been enough. But scientific ability without the voice would also not have been sufficient. The voice, added to reason and knowledge, dominated committees in a degree that reason and knowledge alone could not have achieved.

"I'm surprised to find you welcoming radioastronomers up here on your mountain, Dr. Almond. Isn't it going to put quite a bit of strain on your resources?" began Cameron.

"It would put a worse strain on my public relations if I didn't."

"I suppose you know why I'm out here?"

"Of course. To report on the viability of two schemes, one British and one Australian. You and Dr. Nygaard. Is he coming along for dinner, by the way? I hear he's a bit under the weather."

"I don't know. Perhaps we should find out."

Mrs. Hambly then intervened to say that the "poor gentleman" wouldn't be along to dinner, that she'd taken him some soup and a few other things, and would they like to begin dinner now.

"I won't say no to that. A long night ahead." Almond grinned. "By the way, let me introduce these chaps. Dr. Cameron—Ly Davis from Sydney, Tom Cook and Bill Gaynor from the U.K. on the British forty-eight-inch, the rest from Canberra—Jim Tucker, Alf Maddocks and John Weymore. Well, that's the introductions. How about a spot of wine?"

The dinner passed quickly, most of the men being keen to get to their respective telescopes, to make sure all preparations for the night's work were in hand. They filed out one by one, leaving Almond and Cameron lingering over the coffee.

"I really should be going too, but I wanted to have a bit of a chat. If you're off in the morning there won't be another opportunity," explained Almond.

"Obviously you're interested in the new radiotelescope—naturally. For me you'll understand that it's still *sub judice*. Even so I'd be glad to hear anything you've got to say about it. About the wind up here, for instance."

"Ah, you've already spotted that," Almond said, nodding.

"Of course. It howled around like a banshee last night."

"Frankly, I can't see it. They've got problems down on the plain, they've got problems up here on the mountain, and they've got design problems as well. Scientifically it would all make a lot more sense in Chile."

"Couldn't you say that about the 150-inch?"

"Oh, I've always thought it a tossup so far as the 150-inch is concerned. It's a question of trading the political stability of Australia against the astronomical advantages of Chile."

"Why is it different for a radiotelescope?"

"Because this particular radiotelescope costs much less than the 150-inch."

"So the financial risk in Chile isn't so important."

"Right."

"Suppose a case were made for a much smaller dish at higher frequency?"

"Ah, that really would be different, wouldn't it?"

"In what way?" Cameron finished the coffee with his usual quick snap, as if drinking whisky.

"Well, first it would be more interesting—from my own point of view. It touches much more closely on the sort of work we're doing."

"Interstellar molecules?"

"Gas and molecules. And of course a smaller dish would be a smaller operation."

"So you'd prefer it?"

"Yes. Frankly, yes. But in saying that perhaps I'm following my own interest too closely."

"There are quite a few other people who seem to like the idea."

Almond thought for a moment. "I think most people except the radioastronomers would prefer it."

Cameron waited for Almond to extend this seeming paradox.

"Radioastronomers aren't too happy with the new techniques needed for these very high frequency receivers. Radioastronomy has always been firmly based on the kind of electrical engineering which led to radar. This is something different, more in the solid-state field, a kind of uneasy mixture of solid state with advanced electronics. Not many people are at all comfortable with it."

"I wouldn't have though it too bad," said Cameron with a frown. This was a new point of view.

"Not for you people in nuclear physics perhaps," answered Almond, "but bad for astronomers. Astronomy is trailing five to ten years behind nuclear physics. I'll take you down to the 150-inch in a moment. You'll find it all computer controlled. You'll find a lot of our output digitized. It's all the sort of thing you people in nuclear physics learned to do ten years ago. We're catching up fast but we've had a century or more of prejudice to cope with. So it takes time."

Almond stood up, evidently ready to start his night's work. Cameron followed outside the lodge. Away from the lights, in a little clearing in the woods, the two men looked up at the sky.

"Know the southern sky at all?" asked Almond.

"No, but then I can't say I know the north either. Except the obvious things like the Plow."

"It's rather strange but we don't have that kind of distinctive constellation in the south. Our constellations are mostly chains of stars, like Centaurus far over in the west, and Hydra, which is down now. The difference is a bit like the two sides of the moon."

"How's that?"

"Well, there are no big dark maria on the other side of the moon, the side we don't see from the earth."

"Any reason?"

"There's a chap in America who claims he understands it. I'm sure I don't."

Cameron remembered something in his conversation with Nygaard. It was characteristic of Cameron that odd details would recur to him, as if they needed to be fitted into an ordered pattern in his brain.

"When I was going into this high frequency business—if I may come back to it—the point was made to me that a forty-foot dish here on Mount Bogung would put the thirty-six-foot on Kitt Peak out of business. Back in the U.K. someone made the same point—about the south here being much better. Why would that be?"

A gust of wind blew up. Cameron could see his companion's hair rising like a great mop.

"Oh, because of the center of the galaxy. It's the richest store of molecules, and it passes almost overhead. Look!"

Almond pointed up at the Milky Way. Cameron could see it like a great arch across the sky, passing high through the zenith. He noticed a bright red star in the direction Almond was pointing. "What's that?" he asked.

"It must be Mars. I never know exactly where the planets are—we don't work on them here. But you can tell because it's red and bright. How about coming to the big dome tonight? Best later on. I have to get my program ready now, but if you were to come along soon after midnight I could show you the telescope. We stop for a snack at about that time."

Almond was gone away into the darkness. I'll just bet they stop for a snack, thought Cameron. Perpetually eating, these damned astronomers. He gazed up at the Milky Way again. Then he walked a half mile or so from all manmade lights, from the lodge and from the surrounding houses of the observatory staff. The sky was darker now, with stars powdered everywhere across it. He looked up at Mars again, and as he did so an odd quirk stirred once more in his brain. A detail out of place. It seemed silly, but then he was getting very tired. Best to go back to his room and to snatch some sleep. Damn

65

the conference tomorrow and damn the astronomers' midnight picnic.

The wind was blowing hard as he made his way back to the lodge. Before settling in for the night he returned to the common room and began searching a newspaper which he had looked through earlier in the day. Repeatedly he skimmed the pages without finding the part he was seeking. The sound of a nose violently blown made him swing around.

"I think I've got it licked," muttered Nygaard. He was clad in slacks and a huge sweater with a scarf half covering his face. In one hand he carried a box of tissues, in the other a soup bowl and an empty cup and saucer.

"I thought I'd return these," he said, indicating the crockery. "What were you looking for?"

"The astrology page," answered Cameron.

"I've no wish to have my horoscope cast just at this moment in time."

Then Mrs. Hambly came in and swept up the crockery. She asked Nygaard if there was anything else he wanted.

"Only the astrology page from the newspaper, if you've got it, Mrs. Hambly."

Mrs. Hambly's face shone like the morning sun; at last here was a "gentleman" who understood the more important aspects of astronomy. In a moment she was back from the kitchen with the missing sheet from the newspaper. Cameron, irritated with himself for not guessing the obvious, marveled once again at the instant adaptability of Americans. How had Nygaard managed to dig that scarf thing out of his luggage? What the devil had led him to think he might need it?

In a moment Cameron had found what he wanted—his memory wasn't playing him false after all.

"It says here that Mars is in Taurus."

"Why shouldn't it be?"

"Is the center of the galaxy in Taurus?"

66

"My god, no! It's in Sagittarius, miles away from Taurus."

"That's what I thought. If you step outside you'll find Mars is in Sagittarius."

"Then the gook who writes that astrology column has got it wrong."

The inconsistency in Cameron's mind came into focus.

"You know, Nygaard, it's always been my observation that cranks are uncannily accurate about details. Cranks are always trying to explain why the atomic constants have the values we find them to have—or why the orbits of the planets have the sizes we observe them to have. If a crank quotes for you the semi-major axis of the earth's orbit you can bet your bottom dollar he's got it right to five decimal places. I'll bet the average professional astronomer couldn't get it right straight off to three decimal places."

"So what?"

Cameron held up the newspaper. "If this thing says Mars is in Taurus I'd expect it to be in Taurus."

Nygaard gave a croaking laugh and sniveled into his tissues. "You've got it wrong, Cameron. The chap who writes that astrology rubbish isn't a crank. He's a hard-headed pro. He knows the kind of ass-headed public he's dealing with. He couldn't care less whether Mars is in Taurus or in Timbuktu."

"I walked along the road, maybe for a half a mile. To get away from the lights," Cameron said slowly. "There was something funny about it."

"Funny."

"Fuzzy would be a better word. You know, Nygaard, I've always had particularly good eyesight. At my age it begins to go off a bit, but not for this kind of thing. Mars looked slightly fuzzy. Maybe that's what started me on this track."

Cameron lifted the paper again. Nygaard shrugged. "Well, it's easy to go out and take another look, isn't it?"

They walked about a hundred yards away from the lodge and

gazed out toward the west. The bright red starlike object had moved perceptibly toward the horizon since Almond and Cameron had first seen it.

"Looks O.K. to me," said Nygaard.

Cameron forbore to point out that what with all the sneezing and blowing anything at all might be expected to look O.K. "Let's go on a bit," he said.

They walked for several minutes, past the British forty-eight-inch telescope on the left to the bottom of a gentle decline of the road. A pickup truck came past and its glaring lights destroyed their dark adaptation. They moved away from the road into the bush a little way, and waited.

"Still looks O.K. to me," grunted Nygaard.

"No. I can see it again," Cameron stated firmly. "It's not exactly fuzzy. More like a point of light with a faint halo around it."

Nygaard grunted again and then burst out suddenly, "Hey, wait a minute. The center of the galaxy is in declination twenty-nine degrees south, or thereabouts. O.K.? The maximum declination south of the sun is about twenty-three and a half degrees. O.K.? If the orbit of Mars were in the same plane as the sun it would be just the same for Mars. O.K.? So the question is: Can the orbit of Mars be tilted by as much as five degrees? Or isn't that the center of the galaxy we're looking at?"

"I don't know, except Almond said it was."

"Yeh, but why didn't Almond spot the discrepancy?"

"He said he wasn't interested in planets."

"Neither am I. But I'm interested a lot in the center of the galaxy. I've worked on it often enough."

"Don't you *know*?"

"Well, look, you don't set a telescope on some object by using your *eyes*. If you go along to the big dome you'll find they simply punch the position on a card. The card goes into a computer, and then the computer instructs the telescope where to point. It's all automatic."

"You mean an astronomer doesn't need to know *anything* about the sky?"

"Nothing at all. He simply takes the position of the object he wants to study and pushes it into the computer."

"Where does he get the position from?"

"Out of a catalogue. He'll have a detailed map of the bit of the sky he's interested in though, but only a small bit. You never bother with the whole thing."

"Where does he get the map from?"

"Usually from a special survey of the sky, the whole sky."

"Ah!"

"That's what those two British chaps are doing, making a survey."

"Then they're the chaps we ought to be talking to," said Cameron, still gazing at the red star.

"There's no guarantee they'll know more about it than we do. They only move the telescope automatically from one area of sky to another."

"We can try."

"Yes, I'd like to know about the inclination of Mars. I'm surprised it's as much as five degrees."

"One of them was called Cook. I can't remember the name of the other one."

They stumbled in the bush for a few minutes before reaching the white dome of the forty-eight-inch Schmidt telescope. Nygaard banged on an outer door. Nobody came, so, finding the door unlocked, they gingerly went inside. Everywhere was dark. Not wanting to switch on a light and perhaps ruin an exposure, they groped their way slowly up a stairway.

"What the hell is it?" exclaimed a startled voice above them. Nygaard gave a loud sneeze, which Cameron thought would not improve the composure of the voice's owner. At length, after

Nygaard had cleared his head with a frenzy of blowing, the voice continued in a recognizably Yorkshire accent: "Nearest 'ospital is on t'other side of th' road."

"D'you know the inclination of the orbit of Mars?" wheezed Nygaard.

Cameron heard muttering in the blackness above and the Yorkshire voice suddenly roared out, "Hey, Tom, we've got a right lunatic down here. He wants to know the inclination of the orbit of Mars." A faint light appeared. Cameron continued up the stairs with Nygaard behind. Two white blotches looked down on them, which Cameron took to be the faces of the two observers.

"Ah, it's Dr. Cameron," said a second voice.

"Lunatic or not," answered Cameron, "I'd like to know where Mars is supposed to be."

"We haven't got an almanac. There's one in the big dome. We've only got a few reference books here."

"Let's see if we can find the inclination of Mars," persisted Nygaard.

"What the devil d'you want to know the inclination of Mars for, at this time of night?"

"Is it as much as five degrees?"

"I shouldn't think so. But we can find out."

One of the white faces proceeded to lead them back down the stairs. In a few moments they were in an office where a brighter light could be used. Without explanation, Nygaard looked over a bookcase screwed against the far wall. In a moment he had grabbed one of the books and was flicking through the pages.

"One degree, fifty-one minutes," he croaked in triumph eventually. "Ah, and the longitude of the ascending node—almost fifty degrees. This couldn't make more than about one degree difference—in the dec I mean."

"What's all this in aid of?" asked the observer whom Cameron supposed to be Tom Cook.

"You'd better come and see for yourself," answered Cameron.

Outside and away from the building, Nygaard pointed to the west. "Damn strange. I'd swear that's plumb on the galactic center, declination twenty-nine. So how can Mars be there?"

Cook looked for a while. "It may be some sort of illusion, but it does look funny. Best if we take a look at the N.A. I'll come over with you. Bill can watch the telescope."

"Bill?"

"Bill Gaynor."

"Ah, yes, Bill Gaynor," said Cameron, glad that he'd managed to get two more names straight.

All doors into the big dome were kept locked at night, but Cook had a key to one of them. He led Nygaard and Cameron across a vast ground floor strewn with mechanical equipment. They took a lift up to the second floor, where they emerged, not at the telescope itself, which was still higher in the building, but at a floor occupied by a group of offices and by several photographic darkrooms. There was also a library. After consulting the Nautical Almanac for a moment, Cook exclaimed, "Mars is in right ascension four hours."

"Where's that?" asked Cameron.

Cook returned to the Almanac for a moment. "Taurus," he replied.

"Apology, sackcloth and ashes," moaned Nygaard and then sneezed mightily.

Cameron pointed to a phone. "How do I reach Dr. Almond?"

"Best to call the night assistant. You press the button—here."

A moment later the other two heard Cameron say, "Would you ask Dr. Almond to come immediately to the library? The second floor—yes. No. I don't care if he's in the middle of an exposure—this is a matter of great urgency. Yes—immediately. Tell him this is Dr. Cameron."

Almond appeared ten minutes later. He came into the library with scarcely disguised truculence, as if to show that he would

71

need a mighty good reason for having his night's work so rudely interrupted.

"I said after midnight," he exclaimed peremptorily to Cameron.

"*Calm down, little man.*"

"What's that?"

"The object you thought was Mars isn't Mars. I thought you might be interested, but if ye're not then away back to your spyglass."

Cameron was well aware of the extent to which big instruments dominate the men who use them. This was something he'd never liked. He saw it in Almond now and this caused him to react.

Almond, for his part, had felt that Cameron had gone unreasonably beyond his invitation by summarily removing him from the telescope. Maybe he had been wrong. Very simply, he asked, "How do you know?"

"Mars is in R.A. four hours, Dr. Almond."

Tom Cook held out the Almanac, which Almond studied for a while.

"So Mars and the galactic center are practically in opposition, not conjunction," added Cook.

"That's certainly what it seems to be. Let's go outside and take a look."

Once again Cameron found himself gazing at the western sky, out in the direction of the great Australian desert. The others were murmuring in excitement now.

"It's a supernova," exclaimed Almond. "A supernova close to the center of the galaxy."

There was a long silence broken again by Almond. "That thing will be down in an hour. I know what I'm going to do. I'm going to get a spectrum." Then, turning to Cook, he went on, "You can do what you like, Tom, but if I were in your shoes I'd get an E plate of that chap before you lose him."

72

The party dissolved in a flash, leaving Cameron alone. In particle physics there is no flurry and excitement over getting results. The results in the end can be exciting enough, but getting them is a long and often tedious business. Hundreds, perhaps many thousands of bubble chamber films may have to be taken and then subjected to careful measurement and computer analysis. So, unlike Almond, Cameron had no instinct to rush back to the telescopes. Instead he made his way to the lodge. He found Mrs. Hambly on the point of retiring for the night. He asked her how he should go about making coffee, because he thought the others might be along in an hour or so for a special conference. But Mrs. Hambly would have none of his making the coffee. She insisted on waiting herself. Cameron lit a big log fire. Then he persuaded Mrs. Hambly to produce a spot of Scotch. Toasting his feet, drinking the whisky, he found some satisfaction in the night's work. His instinct had been right. Perhaps it was just that his eyesight was still very good.

7

The Supernova?

The others returned to the common room in ones and twos. By half an hour after midnight they were all there, nine including Almond, Nygaard and Cameron. Three observations of the object at the galactic center had been made. The color of the object had been measured photoelectrically on one of the small telescopes. Cameron gathered it had a B—V of + 1.7. This apparently meant that the thing was very red, which Cameron could have told them anyway. Almond had "got" his spectrum. He put it on a viewing stand which Cook and Gaynor had brought with them. The spectrum was on a strip of glass about six inches long. The astronomers gathered excitedly around.

"Completely continuous, no lines," exclaimed Almond in high spirits. Cameron couldn't understand this intense display of enthusiasm.

"You mean it's void of information," he said.

"Not at all," roared Almond. "It's like a supernova spectrum. So we know it's a supernova. If it were Mars we'd see reflected sunlight, with Fraunhofer lines."

Then Gaynor put a very large square glass plate on the stand. It measured roughly a foot to the side.

"It's poor quality," explained Cook, "because we got it just above the horizon."

The plate from the forty-eight-inch Schmidt was grossly over-exposed so far as the object itself was concerned. The photographic image had spread until the thing had become a big rough splotch several millimeters across. But in spite of its imperfections as an astronomical plate Cameron could see a wholly strange aspect to it. Not in the thing itself but in the surrounding field. Without hesitation, he shooed the astronomers aside like so many chickens and bent his head over the viewer.

"These are stars?" he asked.

"Yes, you can tell by the grainy structure," answered Cook.

"Ordinary stars?"

"In the nucleus of the galaxy the density of stars is very much higher than it is anywhere else," explained Almond.

"Yes, but you can see many more stars immediately surrounding the thing than you can see further out."

The plate was bright with stars around the thing, but much fainter further out, as Cameron had remarked.

"There's your halo, Cameron," said Nygaard.

"But doesn't that mean we're looking through some sort of a *hole?*" Cameron persisted.

"Exactly." Almond nodded. "We're lucky. There happens to be a hole in the direction of the supernova. Otherwise it wouldn't be so bright."

"I see. There happens to be a hole," grunted Cameron.

"Well, let's do a bit of a calculation," went on Almond. "The thing must have magnitude about minus two. We haven't measured it yet, but it must be about minus two, just because I mistook it for Mars."

"And Mars is about minus two," interjected one of the astronomers.

"The distance modulus of the galactic center is about plus fifteen, which makes the supernova minus seventeen. And that's about right. Perhaps a bit on the low side, but about right," concluded Almond.

"It'll probably brighten up a magnitude or two, Dr. Almond," added Cook.

"I wouldn't be surprised."

"So you think it checks—on there being a window?"

"Obviously. Normally there'd be obscuration due to dust, by anything from four to eight magnitude." Almond rubbed his hands. "This is just what we've been waiting for. Now we can make the 150-inch pay really big dividends." He paused for a moment and then concluded, "But the SN is down now, so I see no reason why we shouldn't go back to our normal observing schedule. We can't do anything more about this thing until tomorrow."

Within a few minutes they were all gone from the common room, back to the telescopes, except for Nygaard and Cameron. Nygaard's cold seemed mysteriously to have vanished, so perhaps there was something psychosomatic in it after all.

"How about a drop, to make you forget that cold?" asked Cameron, pouring whisky generously into two glasses.

"Well, maybe. But I'm feeling better now. I didn't think it would last overly long."

"Why did they all go rushing back to their telescopes just now?"

"I'm rushing back to mine," answered Nygaard, "just as soon as this bloody conference is through."

Cameron snorted. "In physics," he said, "we *plan*. We plan months ahead, years ahead. The experiments we want to do might demand an entirely new machine. It may cost hundreds of millions of dollars and we may have to petition a dozen governments for a year, for two years, for three years, to get it. You astronomers don't plan, you rush around like a chicken without a head. Observe and observe and observe and all shall be revealed unto you."

"Which isn't altogether a bad idea."

"As long as it isn't wholly naïve."

"Meaning what?"

"Meaning the universe isn't something simple, like a clock, where all you have to do is to wrench the back off to see how it works. If you're to understand the universe there are times when you must sit back for a while and *think*."

"I still say meaning what?"

Cameron finished the whisky with a gulp. "Meaning I don't believe Almond's nonsense about that hole. It just happened, didn't it? I suggest, if you find sleep difficult to come by, you spend an odd hour thinking about *how* it happened."

"I don't get it."

"Neither do I, and that's why I'm *thinking* about it."

Cameron wondered about another whisky, decided against it, took his leave of Nygaard with little ceremony and returned to his room. He was soon into bed and once again was almost instantly asleep.

The following morning Nygaard and Cameron were the only ones to breakfast, the others being in bed following their night's work. A car took them back to Wombat Springs and thence to the little upland airfield, where the plane for Sydney was waiting. There were plenty of seats so they took two side by side. When the plane was airborne, Cameron said, "I forgot to ask the scale of that plate."

"Which one?"

"The big one."

"If it's the same as the Palomar survey it's about one minute of arc to a millimeter."

"And that hole of theirs—what would you say?—a couple of centimeters across?"

"I suppose."

"So the hole was about twenty minutes of arc?"

"Something like that."

Cameron glanced at a sheet of calculations he had made in the hour before breakfast.

"What's the idea?" asked Nygaard.

"Only doodling. What I'm really wondering is whether we could find any other photographs, earlier photographs, of that hole."

"You mean *before* the supernova."

"Yes."

"That's a good idea, Cameron. The Palomar survey might just go as far south as this, probably does. In any case there must be some old Harvard patrol plates. Yes, and the New Zealanders—with the Lick people—finished a survey a year or two ago. I should think we could dig up something when we get to Sydney."

"We might have dug something up last night, if only they hadn't all gone rushing back to their telescopes."

"I'm not letting that pass, Cameron, not this morning. I'm feeling better than I was last night. Let me fill you in on the way it is with a big telescope. Start with 365 nights in the year. O.K.?"

"I accept that."

"Even on the best possible site, anywhere on the earth, only about one night in four is really first-class in quality. So straight-away you come down to only ninety really good nights, ninety in a year. O.K.?"

"Go on."

"For delicate work, work on faint distant objects, you can't do anything when the moon is up. So again you have to cut out moonlit nights, which brings you down to forty-five nights. Maybe if you include what astronomers call 'gray time' you could say sixty nights. With only ten astronomers working under really good conditions—well, the ration is only six nights in a whole year. Can you wonder they try to squeeze every minute of it?"

Cameron paused for a moment and then said, "I should have thought it all the more necessary to plan very carefully."

Feeling he wasn't making progress, Nygaard decided to return to the supernova. "It won't be easy to check up on that hole."

"Why not?"

"We didn't get a precise position. Without a position it would be worse than hunting for a needle in a haystack. Best to phone the Observatory. They could measure up the Schmidt plate."

"They could, but they won't."

"Why not?"

"Because they'll be asleep—or eating," said Cameron grumpily.

"You're in a devil of a humor—if I may say so."

"I know. But I feel uneasy."

"Uneasy? Why?"

Cameron simply shrugged.

A car was waiting at the old Mascot airport. It took some time, driving through an intricate maze of streets, to cross the city from the south side of Sydney Harbor to the north. Eventually they made faster progress on a wider thoroughfare, reaching the suburb of Epping just before 1 P.M. Their destination was the headquarters of the C.S.I.R.O. Radiophysics Division in Epping. They were immediately taken to the office of the director, Dr. Wallis, a big, heavy, sleepy-eyed man, who reminded Cameron of Fielding.

"Glad you gentlemen are here at last. This is quite something, isn't it?"

"You've heard about it?" asked Nygaard.

"The supernova? Of course. We had news from Mount Bogung. Everybody's talking about it. We've had the press and radio in our hair all morning. They want to know what we're doing about it."

"You should be observing it," said Cameron.

"There's a strong ground swell in that direction among my chaps," agreed Wallis. "We've been wondering about the conference."

"Wondering what?"

"Well, it's a bit of an embarrassment, Dr. Cameron. Considering the trouble you and Nygaard have been put to—coming all this way—but it doesn't make too much sense, sitting around for two days talking about a telescope we won't be getting for two years—"

"When you might be *observing*," finished Cameron.

"Exactly. Something like this only happens once in a thousand years."

"Frankly, I'd sooner make the trip to Australia a dozen times —later on—than sit around on my fanny now missing all the action," Nygaard stated emphatically.

"You'll want to catch the night plane then?" Wallis asked.

"Right."

"Good. My suggestion is this: We'll go out now with a few of my chaps for a leisurely lunch. While we're out, one of the girls will book space for you. If you'll leave your tickets we'll take care of everything."

After lunch Cameron made a sudden decision. "I'd like to return to Mount Bogung, Dr. Wallis."

"He's got the observing bug," said Nygaard, grinning.

"You're sure you want . . ."

"Of course I'm sure," Cameron asserted.

Wallis looked at his watch and then went to an outer office. In a moment he was back, "There's just time for you to catch the afternoon plane—if you hurry, Dr. Cameron. I've ordered a driver. You'd best start straightaway. We'll book the flight from the office now. Your ticket will be waiting at Mascot."

"I'm sorry to put you to the bother."

"No, no, no. It's we who've put you to bother, coming all this way from England."

"Then I'll say good-bye." Cameron turned to Nygaard. The two men shook hands.

"It's been nice traveling with you," said Nygaard.

"Good observing, when you get back to those telescopes."

"Thank you."

Then Cameron was gone. Nygaard turned to Wallis. "Interesting chap, but awf'ly cantankerous."

"It's his Scottish blood."

"Whatever it is, he's got it. But he did spot the supernova in a queer sort of way."

Throughout the journey back to Mount Bogung, Cameron kept wondering at his sudden change of plan. He had little enough time to spare, chasing up and down Australian bush mountains. Yet somehow he had to find out about the way the galactic center used to look—before this damn thing happened.

Cameron's return wasn't a surprise, because Wallis's office had telephoned Mount Bogung ahead of his arrival. Almond had received the news with mixed feelings. Earlier in the afternoon, over the shortwave radio connecting the Observatory to headquarters in Canberra, there had been a series of messages which had put Almond right out of countenance. Almond was totally fed up with what seemed like a planned invasion of his mountain. The fact that two generous governments had spent ten million pounds on the equipment there made little impression on his mind. Like most scientists who are provided with equipment at great public expense, he regarded the telescope as *his* telescope and the mountain as *his* mountain. He met Cameron on the front steps of the lodge. "Glad to see you back, Dr. Cameron."

"There are a few points I want to check with you, Dr. Almond, before I head back for Europe."

"Scientific or administrative?"

"Scientific. Why administrative?"

"Oh, I thought maybe the British had asked you to act for them."

"They have, on the millimeter radiotelescope."

"I know that; I meant *here*."

"Perhaps you'd better explain."

"Well, we have a fifty-fifty time-sharing agreement. Australian and British."

"I see."

"Obviously it's much easier for us to organize our half."

"Because you're on the spot."

"Yes, especially at a time like this, when there's a fast break."

"They could have people out from the U.K. in what?—forty-eight hours," said Cameron.

"You might think so, but the British work goes through a series of committees. It takes them months to react."

"So what's the trouble?"

Almond waved a sheet of paper. "This. Three people from Pasadena, from the Hale Observatories. They're arriving tomorrow."

"Well?"

"To use British time."

"It seems our people have reacted then."

"I can tell you what they've done," exclaimed Almond in an excited voice. "They've negotiated a time-swap agreement. Observing time here on the 150-inch against time on the Palomar 200-inch. Horse trading!"

Cameron remembered Nygaard's lecture on the scarcity of telescope time, "Well, if this supernova business is too fast-moving for the people in the U.K. to make proper use of their share of the 150-inch, horse trading makes a lot of sense."

"Look," boomed Almond in his richest bass. "This is something for us down here in the south. It's what we've been waiting for. It's why we *built* the telescope."

International cooperation being the lifeblood of Cameron's world, he quite failed to understand Almond's point of view.

"So now we've got sharks from Pasadena," Almond concluded in disgust.

"Why can't they operate on their own telescopes?"

Almond stared in astonishment. "Because of latitude," he said in the tone one might use to a backward child. "The galactic center is in minus twenty-nine degrees declination, Pasadena is thirty-four degrees north. So the center transits sixty-three degrees down from the zenith. And it's worse from their point of view—the thing being low in the evening sky."

Cameron decided to change the subject, "When you got that spectrum last night, did you make a note of the telescope setting?"

"Of course. It's in the observing book."

"Have you checked it?"

"For what?"

"To make sure it really is the galactic center."

"Look. I worked through the night until dawn. After dawn I developed my plates. Then I had five hours' sleep. After that I had breakfast, lingering half an hour over it. Then *this* arrived." Almond waved the sheet of paper once more.

"I'd like to check it," said Cameron firmly.

"Now?"

"Yes. Is there someone who could show me?"

"Oh, I'll take you myself. After all, it was my plate."

Cameron could understand Almond's touchiness. Being responsible for operating any large facility is psychologically wearing. A director has to have eyes in the front and back of the head, front to keep the scientific program in clear view, back to keep watch on the outside world with all its nonscientific motivations and pressures. He could understand Almond's irritation at his own return and at his questions.

Almond led the way to an office on the second floor of the 150-inch building. He opened a somewhat battered brown notebook.

"R.A. seventeen hours, forty-four minutes. Dec minus twenty-eight degrees, fifty-five minutes. That's close to the center. You can take my word for it. But I'll check."

After gazing briefly at a reference book, Almond nodded. "Yes, spot on, within the accuracy of my notes—to a fraction of a minute of arc. I can get it better tonight. Could do it now for that matter."

"Isn't it worth observing in daylight?"

"Not optically. The team from Sydney is working now, in the infrared."

"Wasn't there a survey of the sky, done twenty years ago?"

"The Palomar survey. You know, it might be worth taking a look at the Palomar plate of this region."

Cameron forbore to comment.

It took Almond a few minutes to find the relevant copy of the original Palomar plate. Expertly, he had it on a viewing table, with a low-power magnifier centered on the relevant part of the plate.

"My god!" he exclaimed.

"What is it?"

"There's no sign of the bright halo of stars."

Almond stepped back from the table and Cameron took his turn at the magnifier. It needed no expert eye to recognize an amorphous field, without the slightest sign of the hole which had been so clearly visible on the plate taken the previous night.

"It's happened over twenty years," said Almond slowly. Suddenly he stepped out of the office. Cameron followed him to the library and watched him rifle through a massive volume of photographic prints of the sky.

"The New Zealand survey, made more recently. My god, Cameron, there's no sign of it here either."

Cameron glanced over Almond's shoulder. "When was this taken?"

"I couldn't be sure. A few years ago, I would say, five to ten years."

"So the hole is very recent."

"Yes. I wonder if it could be radiation pressure from the supernova."

Slowly and pensively they made their way to the ground floor and out onto the asphalt area to the south.

"It should be about an hour and a half after meridian passage," muttered Almond, gazing up into the sky. Impulsively he gripped Cameron's arm and exclaimed, "It's there." Following the direction of Almond's arm, Cameron spotted the thing easily. "It's very bright," he remarked.

"Brighter than last night. More like Venus now than Mars. But that's to be expected."

"What?"

"Brightening up. It usually takes about three days for a supernova to come up to maximum."

They found a group of astronomers engaged in excited conversation in the common room. The discussion was technical. Cameron made no attempt to interrupt but contented himself with gathering from the flow of talk what information he could. It seemed the supernova was brightening quite rapidly. This was certainly true in the infrared. Almond told them about the hole, and the radiation pressure idea seemed to find general favor.

"Radiation pressure on what? Gas?" asked Cameron at last.

"Oh, no, dust," exclaimed a young fresh-faced lad, astonished that a distinguished scientist shouldn't know such a simple thing.

"How big are these dust particles?" persisted Cameron.

"Oh, perhaps a tenth of a micron," answered Tom Cook.

"Which would place their masses at what—10^{-15} gram?"

"That sort of thing," agreed Almond.

"I can't see radiation pressure moving particles with such a mass at the speed of light," stated Cameron.

"Nobody was thinking about the speed of light."

"You can't explain this hole except by thinking about the speed of light." Cameron's tone was flat and final now.

"I don't see . . ."

Cameron took up a pad on which somebody had been scribbling. As he was preparing to write, he grunted, "Pity you haven't a blackboard."

"It might be as well to fetch one," said Almond.

So off went two of the observers. Within ten minutes they had a blackboard measuring about five feet by three feet mounted on an easel in the common room. Cameron took a firm stance in front of it.

"First give me some numbers. How big is this opaque region near the galactic center?"

"A kiloparsec."

"That doesn't mean a thing to me."

"10^{21} centimeters. A bit more than that, say 3.10^{21} centimeters."

"How far are we away from the galactic center?"

"3.10^{22} centimeters."

"Good; now I can get started. Draw a sphere of radius r to represent the opaque region and write d for the distance from the center."

Cameron drew the following diagram on the board:

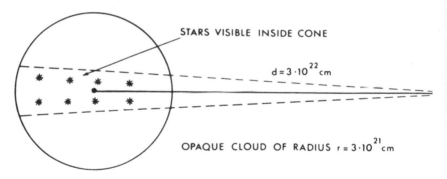

STARS VISIBLE INSIDE CONE

$d = 3 \cdot 10^{22}$ cm

OPAQUE CLOUD OF RADIUS $r = 3 \cdot 10^{21}$ cm

Then he went on: "We're looking into what used to be a part of the opaque sphere, into a hole represented by a cone with a vertex angle of about twenty minutes of arc."

"I don't see why only that cone part of the sphere should have become transparent," said Cook.

"Because at some time there must have been a sudden out-

burst from the supernova. But the opaque dust must be removed at the speed of light. You can't just blow it out by radiation pressure at a smaller speed. A lower speed wouldn't give
this narrow cone, and anyway it would take too long to develop
—it would take at least a time r/v, with v the velocity of the
dust. How fast would you expect the dust to be blown by
radiation pressure?"

"Say one thousand kilometers a second," answered Almond.

"O.K., so the ratio of r to v with $r = 3.10^{21}$ centimeters and
$v = 10^8$ centimeters per second is 3.10^{13} seconds. Which is what?
A million years. So it would take at least a million years to make
a clear hole."

"But why is it so different at the speed of light?" persisted
Cook.

"With everything going at the speed of light, let's ask how
long it takes for an exceedingly narrow cone of essentially zero
angle to develop. Well, just the time it needs for light to travel
from the supernova to us, d/c, with c the speed of light. So
after a time d/c we expect to be able to observe along the
direct line of sight to the supernova. Along the line S to U, like
this."

Cameron drew a second diagram:

S ≡ SUPERNOVA   U ≡ US
d = DISTANCE SU = $3 \cdot 10^{22}$ cm
θ = ANGLE BETWEEN AU and SU = 10 ARC MINUTES

"Now let's ask how long it will be before it becomes possible
to observe a star at A. The answer is the distance S to A plus

the distance A to U divided again by c $(SA + AU)/c$. By Pythagoras' theorem we have

$$SA^2 = SN^2 + AN^2, AU^2 = NU^2 + AN^2.$$

For a narrow cone, AN is necessarily a small distance compared to NU, so that

$$AU = NU + \tfrac{1}{2}\frac{AN^2}{NU},$$

accurately enough. And provided the point A is placed so that SA is large compared to AN we have

$$SA = SN + \tfrac{1}{2}\frac{AN^2}{SN},$$

also to sufficient accuracy. Hence

$$SA + AU = NU + SN + \tfrac{1}{2}\frac{AN^2}{NU \cdot SN}(NU + SN)$$
$$= d\left(1 + \tfrac{1}{2}\frac{AN^2}{NU \cdot SN}\right)$$

Dividing by c, we find that light from the star at A arrives at U (Us) a time

$$\frac{d.AN^2}{2cNU \cdot SN}$$

after the light of stars along SU first reached U. Writing this time difference as δt we have

$$c\delta t = \frac{d\, AN^2}{2 \cdot NU \cdot SN}.$$

At this stage we should notice that

$$\theta = \frac{AN}{NU}$$

is the half angle of our cone, so that

$$c\delta t = \tfrac{1}{2}\, d\, \theta^2. \frac{NU}{SN} = \tfrac{1}{2}\frac{d^2}{r}\, \theta^2,$$

88

again to an adequate approximation. Here we must measure θ in radians. For a cone of half-angle about ten minutes, θ^2 is about 10^{-5}, and with the ratio $d/r = 10$, we get

$c\delta t = \frac{1}{2} 10^{-4} d$.

Finally, putting $d = 3.10^{22}$ centimeters we arrive at

$c\delta t$ about 10^{18} centimeters."

Cameron had barely finished the calculation when a voice burst out:

"That's just about a light-year."

"Which means," concluded Cameron, "that it would take about a year for the hole to open up."

"Very good, Cameron." Almond had jumped up now from his chair and was marching about the common room. "So this explains how the hole has opened up in the short time which has elapsed since the New Zealand survey." Almond continued to pace the room. "The question now is how can the dust have been removed by something from the supernova which propagates with the speed of light."

"Evaporated," burst out the fresh-faced lad. "It must have been evaporated by the flood of radiation from the supernova."

There was an immediate exhilaration among the astronomers, as there always is among scientists whenever a component of the truth has been glimpsed. Everyone drank a glass of beer in a long moment of mental relaxation. Then Mrs. Hambly had the evening meal in front of them. At first they ate slowly and thoughtfully, but quite suddenly everyone seemed to be in a hurry to return to his instruments. Cameron borrowed a set of keys from Almond, so that he could prowl around the various domes as the spirit listed. "But don't go switching on lights at random," cautioned Almond.

It was immediately clear, as soon as they glanced toward the galactic center in the darkening western sky, that the thing had brightened considerably since the preceding evening. Cameron thought Almond had been right in comparing it with Venus, instead of with Mars. Besides being brighter, it was less red now, and this also was more like Venus than Mars.

Cameron did indeed prowl from one instrument to another. He was interested now in what the observers were finding. But there was a limit to the information he could glean at any one of the telescopes. Then he would simply move on to make a nuisance of himself at the next dome. By midnight the galactic center had set once more below the western horizon and everyone could relax again. They met in one of the rooms on the second floor of the big 150-inch dome. A night assistant had warmed some soup. After the first mouthful, Almond said, "I've hit a snag."

"What would that be, Dr. Almond?" asked Tom Cook.

"I don't think the supernova radiation would be strong enough to evaporate the dust."

"How d'you figure that?"

"Like this. Last night we set the magnitude at minus seventeen, but I'll take minus twenty now."

"Because it's brightened up?"

"Yes. Remember the sun is minus twenty-seven about."

"At the earth's distance?"

"Right. So I reckon the supernova would seem about as bright as the sun does from the earth, if the supernova were viewed from a distance of roughly one parsec."

"What the devil is a parsec?" broke in Cameron.

"Roughly three light-years, 3.10^{18} centimeters."

"Thank you. Go on."

"So at a distance of one parsec you'd expect dust particles to be about as hot as the earth—about three hundred degrees K. Not enough to evaporate 'em."

"Unless they were ice and not silicates," argued Cook.

"Yes, but we're not dealing really with one parsec. We've got evaporation over hundreds of parsecs. So even ice wouldn't do."

"Then there's another difficulty, Dr. Almond," broke in the fresh-faced youth.

"How's that?"

"It's a bit hard to explain but it's connected with the time sequence of events. Dr. Cameron explained the formation of the hole by supposing a sudden outburst from the supernova. He found the hole would take something like a year to form."

"To us," added Cameron. "Looked at from other directions in the galaxy the hole would be different."

"O.K., but your first outburst—the one leading to the evaporation of the dust—wouldn't that have to be about a year *before* the outburst we're observing now?"

"I would think so," answered Cameron.

"Then why didn't we see it?"

There was a long silence broken eventually by Cook. "Because at that time the dust wasn't evaporated."

"That's partly true," admitted the lad, "but *something* should have been seen, when the dust had partially cleared."

"He's right," grunted Cameron. "There have to be two outbursts, separated by about a year. For some reason the first one wasn't seen—although it managed to evaporate the dust."

On this mysterious note the group broke up, the observers going back to their instruments. Cameron spent the next couple of hours browsing in the library. Then as the library clock was showing 2:35 A.M. he decided to go back to the lodge and sleep.

It wasn't until noon that he awoke. After shaving and taking a shower and dressing, he went to the common room for the astronomers' breakfast. He had been amused to find that, although observers took the first meal of the day at lunchtime, they nevertheless treated it as breakfast, eating bacon and eggs, toast and marmalade. He could see that Almond was pleased about something. When he asked, Almond grinned. "The Pasadena people . . ." began.

"They're not coming?"

"Not till tomorrow. They got the day wrong. I'll bet someone forgot the international date line."

The fresh-faced lad had come in now. "Have you had any more thoughts, Dr. Cameron?" he asked.

"I was looking up a few things, after you went back to your telescopes last night," began Cameron. "As far as I can see, the total amount of dust to be evaporated isn't so very much."

"How d'you mean?"

"Well, if you projected the whole of it . . ."

"*Before* it was evaporated?" interjected Almond.

"Right. If you projected the whole of it onto a plane you wouldn't have more than 10^{-3} to 10^{-4} grams of it per square centimeter."

Almond nodded. "That's about right," he agreed.

"Well, you don't need too much in the way of high-speed particles to knock that amount of dust into atoms."

"Particles near the speed of light?"

"Yes, relativistic. I reckon a total particle energy of about 10^8 ergs per square centimeter would do it."

"I see. Well, the opaque sphere you were talking about yesterday—that was what? 3.10^{21} centimeters in radius, which gives a projected area of something like 10^{43} square centimeters. So you'd need 10^{51} ergs in your first outburst—10^{51} ergs in the form of relativistic particles," concluded Almond.

"Is that too much?" asked Cameron.

"It's within the accepted range, but it *is* rather a lot."

"Except this supernova does seem unusually bright," interjected Tom Cook.

"Has brightened up still more," announced Bill Gaynor, who had just come in. "Didn't go to bed. I stayed up till it rose—in the east, about an hour ago."

"What is it now?"

"I'd say about minus eight."

There was a whistle around the common room.

"More like a bloody quasar than a supernova," muttered someone.

A long silence followed this remark. It was broken by Almond. "Which would explain something that's been worrying the hell out of me."

"What's that, Dr. Almond?" Gaynor asked, his eyes red with lack of sleep.

"Why the position of the thing is so precisely the same as the galactic center. It's obvious really, isn't it? The center of the galaxy has blown up." Almond's deep voice was grave as he made this pronouncement.

"Like a Seyfert galaxy. My god, we've become a Seyfert galaxy," shouted Cook in apparent delight.

Almond turned again to Cameron, "Yes, and it would make those relativistic particles of yours a lot more reasonable. This *must* be right."

It was just at this point that the mechanic who had driven Cameron around the adjacent countryside came into the common room.

"There's a message for you, Dr. Cameron."

Cameron opened a folded sheet of paper and saw it was a cable from London. It read:

REQUEST YOU RETURN LONDON IMMEDIATELY. NEEDED URGENTLY
FOR MINISTERIAL COMMITTEE OF INQUIRY INTO ENVIRONMENTAL
EFFECTS OF RECENT SUPERNOVA

MALLINSON

93

8

The Quasar

Cameron found there was nothing for it but to take a plane from Sydney to Darwin to Singapore to Bangkok to New Delhi to Teheran to Istanbul to Athens to London, leaving Sydney at 7 P.M. There was nothing quicker than this horrible puddle jumper. To give him the fortitude for such a journey he decided to travel not that day but the next. This at least would give him a chance to rest up a bit. He spent the remaining hours at the observatory in sleeping and in reading from books and periodicals. He made entries and calculations in a hard-bound black notebook which he always carried with him, and he sent two cables to Madeleine, one to Scotland and one to Geneva. The one to Scotland told her to stay in Scotland. The one to Geneva told her to go urgently to Scotland with as little delay as possible.

By the time he left the following afternoon the thing at the galactic center had brightened to a visual magnitude of about minus eleven and it was now very blue. Translated into energy, this meant the thing was emitting some 10^{46} ergs per second in the form of visible light, which would be reasonable if the galaxy was now of the extreme Seyfert kind, indeed approaching a full-blooded quasar. Stated otherwise, the thing had a visual brightness amounting to about one-fifth of the full moon. It shone and sparkled even in full sunlight.

Cameron's journey took rather more than twenty-four hours. His plane touched down at Hearthrow shortly before noon.

"You've cut it pretty fine," Mallinson said outside the customs hall. "The meeting is scheduled for two-fifteen."

It was held at the Department of the Environment. The Minister himself was in the chair. Mallinson apparently was to be secretary. The chairman began by welcoming them all. He went around the table giving names, which Cameron promptly forgot. But he noticed that the committee seemed light on the physics side. In fact the membership was widely scattered—agriculture, environment, medicine, sociology—with a chemist and Cameron himself to represent the physical side apparently. He was fairly sure he could bring the chemist's name to mind if he were really pushed to it. In point of fact he felt awful, just bloody awful.

The committee spent the first half hour discussing its terms of reference. Then they got round to the main item of the agenda, possible environmental effects of the new heavenly apparition, this quasar thing. So the news was out. The thing wasn't a supernova. It was a quasar. The Minister told them he had information from the Royal Greenwich Observatory: the thing had brightened steadily until now it was equivalent to the full moon. Cameron wondered how this was known and then realized the thing would be briefly visible on the southern horizon even from observatories in the U.K. Call the latitude fifty-one degrees north. With the galactic center at twenty-nine degrees south, it would transit ten degrees above the horizon. It wouldn't be "up" for long, but for something as bright as the full moon is wouldn't be hard to make a quick measurement. Cameron wondered why there wasn't an astronomer on the committee, and then remembered the chairman had given some explanation, an apology of some kind.

Now they reached what seemed to be the crux of the meeting, the serious physiological effect of looking at this bright point of light. The man in the street would be only too apt to stare at it in an unguarded way with likely damage to the retina of the eye. It was true the thing was only as bright as the moon, but the moon wasn't concentrated into an extreme point of light. This was the crux of the matter. It was also true the thing was only briefly visible in the late afternoon but they couldn't afford to be complacent on that account. The committee began to discuss the best way to issue warnings to the public and it was agreed these should be implemented immediately. It was agreed that the public be warned not to look toward the thing, except through a piece of exposed film. It was also agreed that commercial makers of film be asked, again as a matter of extreme urgency, to place stocks at the government's disposal.

Throughout this discussion, which he scarcely heard, Cameron had been jotting in his black notebook. Suddenly his attention was jerked back to the meeting by the chairman asking:

"Have you any comments, Dr. Cameron? You haven't given us your views yet."

Even before he opened his mouth Cameron knew his reserve was going to snap, the steely reserve he'd managed to maintain in the presence of the English for so many years. Why were they so smug? Why did they spend such a vast proportion of their time and effort on these outward forms? "I'd like to ask the medical gentleman two places on my right if he would be kind enough to give me a value for the diameter of the entrance pupil of the human eye," Cameron began.

This question took the meeting by surprise. The medical gentleman in question eventually did his best to answer. "Well, it depends a lot on the light intensity. At low intensity it might be as much as a centimeter. In full sunlight it might be as small as one to two millimeters."

"That's what I would have thought. It couldn't by any chance be as large as six inches. That was the reason for my question."

"I don't follow you, Dr. Cameron," said the Minister coldly.

"The wavelength of light is typically about five thousand Angström," Cameron began. "If I take the pupil of the eye to be as much as a centimeter, there are some twenty thousand wavelengths across it. With this number of wavelengths, the eye is incapable of bringing a distant point of light to a focus on the retina to within less than ten seconds of arc. This means the eye is physically incapable of distinguishing between an actual point of light and a disk of light some ten seconds in radius. Such a disk would have a solid angle less than the disk of the sun by a factor of about ten thousand. Since, however, the sun is brighter than the full moon by a factor of about a million, it follows that the illumination of the retina by the quasar will be less than the effect of full sunlight by a factor of a hundred. Therefore the effect of the quasar will not be as deleterious as this committee supposes. In fact the deliberations of the last hour are wrong and irrelevant because this committee does not understand the difference between physical optics and geometrical optics."

"You might have said this *before*," said the Minister, still more coldly.

Cameron rose from his chair. "I am not a teacher of elementary physics," he grunted. "And if I were I would reserve my teaching for students with a reasonable measure of humility. I would not dissipate it on men who set themselves up to advise and control others, but who in fact know little or nothing."

There was a general murmur around the table.

"Quiet," roared Cameron, drawing himself to his full height. "I have spent an hour and a half listening to your drivel. Now you shall listen to me for five minutes. An explosion has occurred in the nucleus of our galaxy. Similar explosions have been observed in many other galaxies. If this particular explosion should turn out to be like one of the smaller ones, the environmental effects on the earth will be comparatively minor. But if it turns out to be one of the larger ones, the whole of our *atmosphere* will be ripped away from the surface of the earth like tissue paper. In not too long a time, gentlemen, you will all be dead, and every other animal, every living thing, will also die." With this awesome pronouncement, Cameron picked up his notebook and briefcase and walked from the room, from the office block, out into the street.

He took a taxi to the Royal Society in Carlton House Terrace. Upstairs on the third floor he tapped on the door to the housekeeper's apartment. His luck was in, for she was able to offer him a room. Unfortunately not one of the best, she explained. This was of small consequence, for it was Cameron's intention to catch the night train to Scotland. It was just sleep he needed through the intervening hours. He paid for the room, so he could leave at any time of his choice. Then he rang Madeleine and was delighted to find her already in Kintail. He told her he would be on the noon train into Kyle of Lochalsh the following day. He threw off his clothes, showered to get some of the appalling journey out of his system, and collapsed into bed— just as he had done on the way out to Australia.

A light tapping on the door caused Cameron to awake. Glancing at his watch, he saw the time was only 6:30 P.M.

"Yes, what is it?" he shouted.

The housekeeper's voice replied, saying there was a gentleman to see him. Cursing that he hadn't gone to a hotel where they couldn't find him, Cameron twisted a dressing gown over his shoulders and yanked the door open with a vicious pull. He found Mallinson standing outside.

"May I come in?"

"I hope it is both urgent and meaningful, Henry."

"The Prime Minister would like to see you."

"Another committee?"

"He has asked you to dinner. I understand there will also be the First Physicist, Sir Arthur Mansfield, and Guy Renfrew, who is the Professor of Radioastronomy at Bristol University."

"That the full crew?" asked Cameron as he started to shave.

"I'm sorry, but your display this afternoon was quite inexcusable."

"*Ah, the poor simple man,*" said Cameron to himself in the mirror.

"And what might that mean?"

"It means you'd better stop playing the fool, Henry. You're likely to be dead in a couple of weeks, man."

"Which makes it all the more necessary to go on behaving in the way I've always behaved."

Cameron finished shaving and began to dress. "There's something to be said for your point of view," he admitted. "But it implies you've always been doing the things you want to do."

"Haven't you?"

"Partly yes, partly no. I've done the things which have been open to me."

"Haven't we all?"

Cameron adjusted his tie and began stuffing his pajamas and toilet articles into one of the bags. He retrieved a shirt and pushed it in as well. Then he followed Mallinson downstairs. There was little prospect of finding a taxi in the rush hour so they left Cameron's bags with the porter and set out to walk the mile or so to Downing Street. Mallinson secured entry into Number 10. When he had passed Cameron to one of the attendants he held out his hand.

"Well, old chap, this may be good-bye."

Cameron gripped the outstretched hand, slackening his grip when he saw Mallinson begin to wince. "I thought you would be staying, Henry."

"Not tonight."

"Then it may really be good-bye. I'm catching the night train."

"I see. How certain can you be about it?"

"Not at all certain. It's more dangerous than I told your committee this afternoon, but it could turn out to be no worse than the risk of serious radiation burns. Try to stay indoors as much as you can. Remember the damaging stuff is quite invisible."

Then Mallinson was gone. Cameron stood there for a while shaking his head. It was a long way back to their student days. It was a short distance into the holocaust which lay ahead. The attendant passed him to a secretary, and the secretary took him upstairs to a room where the Prime Minister was already talking to the First Physicist.

"Ah, Cameron," said the P.M., coming forward.

"You'd like a drink?" he went on after they'd shaken hands.

"Whisky, please."

"Water or ice?"

"Just whisky."

"A Highlander first and last, eh?"

"Something like that."

Cameron shook hands with Mansfield. "I hear you expressed yourself rather freely this afternoon, Cameron," said the First Physicist, a small, bushy man. Cameron had met Mansfield several times before. Just as on those previous occasions, he was now hard pressed not to laugh. Whether it was the man or the absurd title he labored under Cameron couldn't be sure.

"I was tired after thirty hours' traveling," he said by way of explanation.

"Actually it was just as well you did," the Prime Minister remarked. "Otherwise the serious side of this business wouldn't have come to my attention so soon. Often enough it pays to act strongly if you feel strongly, but I don't usually have the courage myself."

Guy Renfrew, the Bristol Professor, was shown in. He was clutching a thin briefcase, which he seemed determined to hang onto for dear life. Renfrew was of medium height, rather solid of build, and younger than Cameron had expected. He wore glasses with steel-rimmed frames which matched his graying hair. He asked the Prime Minister for a sherry, which Cameron always thought of as one of the better forms of mouthwash.

"I thought we'd have dinner first, rather early, say seventhirty. Then we can talk afterwards," explained the Prime Minister.

Throughout the dinner Cameron had his usual distant feeling after traveling, as if his head were floating away into space. He did what he could with the small talk, but it wasn't until the coffee and port were being served that his attention became controlled again. It was the port which brought him up sharp, for Cameron regarded this sweet sickly liquid as one of the seven horrors of the world. He recoiled as the decanter was passed to him by the Prime Minister and quickly thrust it toward Mansfield, who from his avid manner plainly relished the stuff.

"You'd like something else?" asked the observant P.M.

"Not really, Prime Minister. My metabolism is out of joint." Cameron had been sensitive to the remark about Highlanders. He wasn't going to overdo the whisky.

"Then perhaps we can start our discussion. You made certain statements to a meeting this afternoon, Dr. Cameron, which were reported to me. I thought it right to pass your observations to Renfrew and Mansfield."

"I wonder if you'll excuse me while I get my briefcase, Prime Minister?" Renfrew asked.

"Yes, certainly."

Renfrew returned to the dinner table in a moment, clutching his case once again. The others waited while he opened it. He took out several sheets of calculation and an astronomical photograph which he offered to the Prime Minister.

"That's M82, an exploding galaxy. You can see how streams of material have been blown outwards in the polar directions," he began.

"Remarkable," muttered the Prime Minister. "You mean this is the sort of thing which has happened to our own galaxy?"

"Yes, I'd say so."

"You agree, Cameron?"

"No."

"Why not?"

"Perhaps it would be easier for me if Professor Renfrew were to explain just what he's got on his mind," answered Cameron.

"Well, naturally it was Cameron's remark about particles from the center rushing outwards to the solar system and then hitting the earth's atmosphere which caught my attention," began Renfrew.

"Yes?" intervened the Prime Minister.

"If this were happening *in vacuo* then of course it would be the way Cameron says it would. But there is gas, interstellar gas, all along the plane of the galaxy. The gas will act as an effective shield."

"What have you to say to that, Cameron?"

"How much gas? Along a unit column, what? A hundredth of a gram for a column with a cross section of one square centimeter."

Mansfield and the Prime Minister turned toward Renfrew. Cameron sensed Mansfield would simply follow the personal clash between himself and Renfrew. He wouldn't bother too much with the argument itself.

"I wouldn't dissent from that value," Renfrew admitted.

"High energy particles pass very easily through one hundreth of a gram of hydrogen," Cameron said, smiling.

"Ah, yes," Renfrew continued in a raised voice, "but you've forgotten the magnetic field."

"Perhaps you'd better explain for the Prime Minister and Sir Arthur Mansfield why you think a magnetic field changes the problem."

"Relativistic particles which are trying to get out from the center get locked to the gas, by the magnetic field. So an outward beam of particles from the center is forced to carry the gas along with it. This slows the beam down, producing the shielding effect. Look, you can see this is exactly what has happened in M82."

Renfrew held up the photograph, pointing to the polar jets. "The outward beam has been checked here in the plane of the galaxy. So it has been forced to burst out in the polar directions, producing all these jets."

The Prime Minister glanced sharply at Cameron. "You agree, Cameron?"

"No. I said M82 wasn't the same as this thing in our own galaxy."

"Why not?" asked Renfrew in his raised voice.

"The issue is difficult and technical," began Cameron calmly, "but I'll do my best to explain, and I'll ask you all to remember that this question of confining and controlling relativistic particles by a magnetic field is a topic in which I have worked all my life. Professor Renfrew's argument contains a critical assumption—that the current flowing in the ambient gas, the current responsible for the magnetic field, is given and invariable."

"Excuse me . . ." began Renfrew.

"Except insofar as the gas is pushed around by the beam of high-speed particles," Cameron went on. "Such a view is correct if the magnetic inductance of the whole system happens to be large compared to the energy of the relativistic particles. But when the inductance happens to be small compared to the relativistic particles the currents become controlled by the particles, which in effect annihilate the initial currents."

"What happens then?" asked the Prime Minister.

"The high-speed particles stream through the gas just as if there had been no magnetic field."

"Well, then I'll come back to you, Professor Renfrew," the Prime Minister continued.

"I don't see how the currents can be annihilated . . ."

"The precise details of how it happens are complex, just as I said. The simplest way to look at it is like this," Cameron continued remorselessly. "Suppose the beam contains a powerful source of electromotive force. The electromotive force proceeds to cancel the electric fields which were driving the original currents. Then according to Ohm's law the currents fall to zero."

Cameron glanced around the table. Leaning back in his chair, he still continued. "To attempt to control relativistic particles with a magnetic field of small energy tied to a thin gas is as absurd as it would be to attempt to control the explosion of a grenade within a paper bag."

Then he laughed heartily, turning to the Prime Minister. "I think I'll have the drop you were offering me, Prime Minister."

The Prime Minister waved an arm. A glass of neat whisky and a jug of water were quickly placed on Cameron's right. Ignoring the water, he lifted the whisky glass and downed its contents in a single snap. He enjoyed the shocked look on Mansfield's face and watched the fellow with a scarcely veiled contempt as he sipped the horrible sticky port. The Prime Minister stuck manfully to his task, even though he could now see he had a "situation" on his hands.

"But how about this?" he asked, holding up Renfrew's picture of M82.

"This is a case where the inductance is more or less comparable to the relativistic energy, so this case happens to meet the conditions of Professor Renfrew's argument," explained Cameron without the slightest loss of diction. "But anyone who takes the trouble to look up the data, as I am sure Professor Renfrew has done, will discover that this is a mild case. As explosions go it is rather a small one."

"Doesn't look small to me," grunted the Prime Minister.

"Which simply emphasizes the appalling vastness and gravity of the situation in our galaxy." The only effect of alcohol on

Cameron was that his vocabulary tended to become flowery.

"But I still don't see how you can know that our galaxy and M82 aren't similar," said Renfrew.

"At today's meeting I said that *if* the explosion in our own galaxy has been a major one the effects will be catastrophic."

Cameron turned and caught the attendant's eye. He pointed to his glass. Within seconds it was recharged with neat whisky. He knew they were all expecting him to down it in a gulp so he left it sitting there in the glass.

"Besides," he added, "the cosmic ray group at Sydney University has already found the relativistic particles. They're beginning to arrive at the earth. This shows the explosion to have been a major one."

"How did you discover this?" asked the P.M., now in an anxious tone.

"Very simply, Prime Minister. By ringing Sydney University on my last day in Australia. Two young chaps from the group came and met me at the airport. I had a couple of hours with them."

"Did they appreciate the significance of what they were finding?"

"In the environmental sense, not at all."

"Did you tell them?"

"No."

"Thank god for that."

"Why, Prime Minister?"

"Well, at least we won't have a panic on our hands."

Incredible, thought Cameron. They're going to be dead ten days from now, yet all they can think of are the modes and conventions of the past. No panic in the streets, no mobs at the door. He picked up his whisky and held it against an overhead light. They watched, again expecting him to drink it. So he put it down on the table with a bit of a thump and said, "Don't we have a cosmic ray station in this country? Havarah

Park, as I remember. What are the chaps at Havarah Park finding?"

The Prime Minister looked quizzically at Mansfield. Cameron, to his delight, saw Mansfield had never heard of Havarah Park.

"I wonder if I might use the phone, Prime Minister," Cameron said, standing.

"Oh, no, I'll find out," exclaimed Mansfield.

Like a bullet he was out of the room. Cameron noted these were the first words the First Physicist had spoken.

As soon as Mansfield was gone Cameron took up the port decanter, filled Mansfield's glass and passed the decanter to the Prime Minister, "A good drink, Prime Minister, if you have the head for it. But severe on the kidneys."

Cameron could see this simple proceeding had succeeded in stifling some remark Renfrew had been on the point of making. "How are things at Bristol these days, Professor Renfrew? You were at Oxford, weren't you, Prime Minister?"

The Prime Minister, seeing the initiative thus wrested from him, replied, "You won't be thinking about the 1000-Gev anymore, I suppose?"

"I've already crossed that bridge, Prime Minister. A bit like life."

"How's that?"

"Adjusting oneself to the thought the day will inexorably come when one will cease to be. Strange how few people ever manage to cross that particular bridge. They'll be dead now almost before they know it."

"I don't see how you can be sure of that," broke out Renfrew passionately.

"Which is just your trouble, isn't it, Professor Renfrew? You can't cross this particular bridge. You will go on denying the truth until the last syllable of your existence."

"Which is scarcely a polite observation, Cameron," admonished the Prime Minister.

"With death only ten days away, Prime Minister, politeness becomes a meaningless concept."

Mansfield was back.

"Well?" asked Cameron.

"They've been changing the system," he began. Hearing an audible groan from Cameron, he rushed hastily on. "But since this explosion thing happened they've gone back on the air again."

"With what result?"

"I'm expecting definitive news any time now."

Cameron thought about capping this anticlimactic situation by snapping the whisky, but decided a better moment might come later. "Give you time for another glass of port," he observed. Mansfield took the hint and began sipping from his glass.

"How long do you expect this news might take?" asked the Prime Minister.

"Any time," answered Mansfield, staring around vaguely.

Renfrew was clearing his throat and Cameron knew another assault was on the way.

"Even if what Cameron says is all right so far, there's still another question to be answered," Renfrew began.

"How's that?" asked Cameron.

"Look, Cameron, you can hardly maintain that particles travel as fast as light. So particles can't arrive here as fast as the light."

"Omitting Cerenkov situations, I agree."

"Over such a great distance the difference in the speeds of the particles must cause them to arrive at different times."

"Agreed."

"And if the particles hitting the earth are therefore spread out over a long time interval they won't do anything very harmful at all. It's only if they hit the earth as a sudden pulse . . ."

"My god, there's a good point," exclaimed Mansfield.

Cameron stared up into the air for a long time, until he knew he had their attention. "If the energy, which I will call E, of a particle is measured in terms of its rest mass and if E is fairly large, the particle velocity differs only fractionally from the speed of light by $1/(2E^2)$. This means the time of travel differs fractionally by $1/(2E^2)$. The time of travel for light in this particular explosion is about thirty thousand years. So particles will lag behind the light by one year when E is about a hundred, particles will lag by ten days when E is about seven hundred, and particles will lag by only a single day when E is about two thousand."

He turned on Renfrew. "Would you like to check that before I go on?"

Renfrew took out a pen and worked for some time on sheets of paper from his briefcase. "Yes, but how much energy is there at these large values of E?"

"More than you might think," went on Cameron. "The differential energy spectrum of a typical particle distribution is about like $E^{-2.5}$. This means the fraction of the total energy which lies above any particular E goes like $E^{-0.5}$. For an E of one thousand, about one-thirtieth of the total is therefore involved."

"Meaning exactly what?" asked Mansfield.

"Meaning 3 percent of the total flux will arrive at the earth in the next ten days."

"Is that enough?" There was a deep worry line on the Prime Minister's forehead.

"To cause damage?"

"Yes."

"It's certainly enough to cause serious damage, to produce serious radiation exposure hazards, but exactly how far-reaching the final effect will be I do not know—because I don't have a good estimate yet for the total energy of the explosion."

"What are the possibilities?"

"A disastrous upward displacement of the whole of the earth's atmosphere would require a flux of about 10^{12} ergs per square centimeter. For isotropic emission from the explosion, remembering we are situated some 3.10^{22} centimeters from the explosion point, the total at the center of the galaxy would need to be about 3.10^{59} ergs."

"Are you including the 3 percent effect?" asked Renfrew.

"Yes, of course."

"Is that amount of energy possible?" asked the Prime Minister.

"According to the papers I consulted while in Australia, the most powerful explosions in galaxies do exceed 3.10^{59} ergs."

Cameron thought Renfrew might seek to deny this last assertion, but the man seemed sunk now in despair.

"How are we to *find out?*" exclaimed the Prime Minister with some passion.

"By making observations of a kind which can be done at Havarah Park," answered Cameron.

At this point an attendant brought an envelope to Mansfield. He slit it open, took out a sheet of paper, read it, and then said, "It's from Havarah Park! From Professor Albright. He says everything is on the air again, and they're getting splendid results."

"Splendid results!" roared the Prime Minister. "What the devil does he mean by that?"

"Obviously they're getting a powerful flood of particles. But exactly how much—well, I reckon we'd have to go up there ourselves to find out. This isn't the sort of thing I could explain over the telephone," muttered Cameron.

"What's to be done? Make a trip to this Havarah Park place?"

Cameron thought for a moment and then shook his head.

"No, Prime Minister, I was less than accurate in suggesting the idea. It's true we could eventually get the information we need that way . . ."

"Why not . . ."

"Professor Albright's chaps might be able to tell us more or less what's happening down here at ground level. But they'd have to go through a lot of detail—probably involving more measurements—before they could get at what we really need—which is the particle intensity and spectrum at the *top* of the atmosphere." Cameron continued to shake his head. "I think we can get what we want quicker empirically," he added.

"You mean by just waiting," said the Prime Minister in an empty voice.

Mansfield nodded. "That's right, P.M. We'd best suck it and see."

Cameron glanced pointedly at Mansfield and then at Renfrew. "I have to catch the night train for Glasgow, Prime Minister."

The Prime Minister took his cue immediately. "You take my car to Euston, Dr. Cameron—I won't be needing it. Let me see you downstairs."

Leaving Mansfield sipping his port and Renfrew making calculations, Cameron and the Prime Minister walked slowly from the room.

"I'm sorry for my abrupt behavior today, Prime Minister, but it may have saved a day, perhaps two days, in alerting you to what is needed."

"Which is?"

"Protection of the population against radiation damage—in case there's no outright catastrophe."

"Otherwise there's nothing to be done."

"If there were plenty of time you might contemplate a retreat underground. With an adequate supply of nuclear energy it might be possible to ride out a very long siege."

"You wouldn't be interested . . ."

"If there were time, possibly yes."

"You don't think . . ."

"No."

"I might try."

"You probably will, Prime Minister. In a way it's your job to try."

"And you?"

"I wish to spend the last of my days in the land of my forefathers. This may sound darkly Celtic, but depend upon it, Prime Minister, I shall struggle to survive until the ultimate moment, just as my ancestors struggled to survive."

"You seem to take for granted . . ."

"I have a foreboding."

"Darkly Celtic."

"Yes."

The two men shook hands.

"I'm sorry you're going, Cameron. I would have liked you here."

"I'm sorry too, Prime Minister, but my own country has first call—I may be needed there."

Then Cameron was gone, out to the waiting car. He gave the driver instructions to go first to Carlton House Terrace, to pick up his bags, and then to Euston.

An hour later the Glasgow train rolled slowly away. Cameron sank back in his seat, utterly weary, only half realizing he was now crossing a watershed into a wholly new life, in which his technical knowledge as a physicist would be of little account, but in which his practical skill and his heritage would be of overriding importance.

9

The Inferno

Madeleine was waiting at Inverness, not at Kyle as Cameron had expected. She had a pleased little-girl expression, so evidently something favorable had happened. It turned out to be the new Range Rover, which they'd had on order for some months. Cameron looked it over carefully. It was ironic the thing should have been delivered now. Examining the extensive rear of the vehicle he had an idea, obvious really. He and Madeleine went to the Royal Hibernian Bank, where they drew a considerable sum from their account. Then they toured the Inverness shops buying a multitude of stores, until the rear of the Rover was chock-a-block with stuff. Finally, Cameron drove through side streets toward the harbor, to the company which delivered gas into Kintail. He found a driver and tipped him five pounds, with another five to follow, if the fellow would deliver not one big cylinder but a whole truckload of cylinders. Cameron insisted on the delivery that day, not the next day, or the day after, which was the reason for the big tip, he explained.

They started the drive from Inverness to Glen Shiel, much as they had done a month earlier. Was it only a month? A kaleidoscope of faces swam through Cameron's brain—Fielding, Mallinson, Nygaard, Almond and his chaps, the Prime Minister.

It all seemed oddly unreal. The reality lay in Glen Shiel and in the events which the next few days would bring.

"Is it serious?" Madeleine asked.

"Yes, we'll have to stay indoors, because of radiation from the sky. That's why I bought all these stores."

"There are fires everywhere in the south. It was on the news this morning."

"The south?"

"Not the south of England, the southern hemisphere, and in places like California."

"How has it been happening?"

"Fires in the sky. I expect they'll have pictures of it by this evening."

Cameron lapsed into silence while Madeleine drove. He pretended to be dozing off, so that he could think. Fires in the sky meant a lot of energy simply had to be hitting the top of the atmosphere. By a lot he meant something comparable—so far as energy was concerned—with ordinary sunlight. He hadn't thought much about the early stages of it. He'd been concerned all the time about the grimmer prospect of atmospheric stripping. But there would be great storms all right, powerfully electric. Like thunderstorms but on a bigger scale. And it would get very hot. He began to worry about the wooden roof of their house.

There are many streams from the Mam Ratagan ridge down to Loch Duich. One of them ran close by Cameron's house. As soon as he and Madeleine reached home Cameron went off to study the stream, feeling it would be absurd for the house to burn with so much water rushing past it. But without heavy machinery there was curiously little he could do. So after a quick lunch he decided on a different tack. Wearing a metal helmet now, two of which he'd bought in Inverness, he rigged up a length of flexible piping from the kitchen water tap to the roof of the house. Their drinking water came from a spring high up the hill, so there was ample pressure for it to reach the roof. The important thing was to fix the flexible pipe firmly enough at the top, so that it would hold its place even in a high wind. He made a solid job of it, and darkness was falling by the time he'd finished. Then the truck arrived with the big delivery of gas. Cameron gave the driver his second five pounds, Madeleine gave the chap a cup of tea, and the truck was soon turned and away toward Letterfearn. As Cameron settled to a cup of tea and to toasted crumpets, he felt they'd managed their first decisions reasonably well. It occurred to him that it might be just as well to remove the guttering on the roof, or at least to block it up, so that water from his pipe would run everywhere down the outer walls. The sides of the house would then be protected as well as the roof.

The news that night was far from reassuring. Fire storms were already sweeping the whole of the earth, except for a polar cap north of latitude forty-five degrees. This was a direct consequence of the relation of the galactic center to the orientation of the earth. There were fragmentary pictures on TV which immediately convinced Cameron that the energy input at the top of the atmosphere must already be comparable with the solar flux, of the order of 10^6 erg per square centimeter per second. Such an input of relativistic particles would certainly produce devastating atmospheric motions within only a few days. The position was bad, particularly as there must be the wish at top government level to clamp down on the worst aspects of the news.

Cameron spent a couple of hours doing precise health calculations. This was a field in which he had long experience. He found he'd long ago guessed the results instinctively. The relativistic particles hitting the earth must have energies of at least 10^{12} volts, otherwise they wouldn't have reached the earth by now. They would travel essentially straight, without appreciable deflection by the earth's magnetic field. This gave total shielding for terrestrial latitudes north of 61 degrees. Glen Shiel was 57 degrees, which meant that for a short time each day particles would hit the high atmosphere at a flat angle of about 4 degrees. For angles so near grazing incidence the atmosphere would be very opaque. It would be strongly shielding, enough to make special protection against radiation damage hardly necessary.

The situation would be devastatingly otherwise nearer the equator. Owing to electron cascade effects, the electron flux high in the atmosphere would be of the order of 10^9 erg per square centimeter per second. This was ten million times greater than the usually permitted levels. The atmosphere would give some protection at sea level but far too little to save any creatures who were not protected by thick metal shields. The situation would even be quite bad in the south of England. Cameron wondered how far his instinctive realization of these points might have affected his decision not to stay in London. Then he reflected there was little advantage in avoiding a radiation death if the whole atmosphere was soon to become a flaming tornado. The vast populations of the world were already totally doomed, but so would everything be in only a few short days. Life would proceed more or less normally for a little while up here in the north of Scotland. The end would come with a swift finality.

The wind started about nine o'clock. Cameron and Madeleine had gone to bed early. Cameron, after sixty hours of strain, physical and mental, was soon asleep. Yet the strange wind had him awake immediately. It was a wind that hummed, sobbed and whined alternately. Cameron knew immediately what it was. Away to the south the air was being unnaturally heated. The pressure would rise, there would be an explosive expansion toward the north which would overcome the usual inhibiting geostrophic effects. Even while he and Madeleine listened as they lay in bed the wind became ever more shrill. Within half an hour it became a raging gale. Uncannily, the air of this

November night was hot, as if it were being blown from a cosmic furnace.

The timbers were creaking like a ship at sea. Fearful the house might be breached, Cameron and Madeleine dressed themselves as best they could in the dark. The main electric supply was gone already. Cameron knew the wind must be from the south. To the south lay the bulk of Mam Ratagan. So this was the wind on the leeside. What it must be in locations facing directly into the south defeated his imagination. Only the sturdiest of squarely built stone houses exposed to the full fury of the tempest would survive this first assault.

After lying uneasily awake for an hour, listening for incipient damage to the house, they fell asleep again. It was light when Cameron awoke. He found Madeleine in the kitchen cooking breakfast, so the gas supply was still functioning—which he'd hardly expected. The wind outside was still high but the calico-tearing noise had gone from it now. In its exposed northern part the loch was running a vast swell.

The electric supply was still out. Since the cables ran overhead, Cameron had little hope of it ever returning to normal— the wind must have brought it down in a score of places. He asked Madeleine to keep the lids of the deep freeze closed, then ate his breakfast, thinking he'd try to get the old donkey engine working again. It hadn't been used since they'd come onto main supply two years ago.

Cameron swore volubly as he got the bottom half of the heavy engine centered on its concrete bed. He bolted it down and lined up the dynamo section. Standing up and stretching his back, he remembered the last time it was done. By Mac-Tavish, the old chap from Morvich with a goiter. It was fine then, with him the gentleman scientist not needing to soil his hands. He checked with a spirit level, finding the dynamo shaft wasn't right after all. So he had to spend an infuriating hour finding shims to make it balance properly. He was more or less through with it, and checking he was properly stocked with diesel fuel, when he heard an approaching vehicle. Stepping outside the little shed which housed the engine, he found Duncan Fraser getting out of his old Land Rover. Duncan, bent against the wind, came over to join him, "Tom MacLean has had an accident," he said.

"What happened?"

"We were clearing trees off the road. One of them came down on him."

"How bad is he?"

"Not good, Dr. Cameron. I was wondering . . ."

"Yes?"

"He ought to go to Fort William. I was wondering about that new car of yours. . . . He'd be able to lie down in it."

Cameron got into the new car, started it and followed behind Duncan's Land Rover, back along the road to Letterfearn. On the far side of the village he found a small group of men clustered about the unfortunate MacLean. Cameron could see a tree must have fallen across his legs. The others had managed to lever it off with the aid of several good-sized branches. Two women from the village had brought sheets which they somehow had worked under the injured man. As Cameron and Fraser arrived, two of the men were knotting the sheets around two smaller straight branches, so as to improvise a stretcher. Without wasting time for talk, Cameron opened up the back of the Range Rover. MacLean was clearly in serious pain, for he cried out in a shrill voice as they lifted him into the vehicle. Cameron noticed one of the women was Mrs. MacLean, Tom's mother.

"It's better than internal injuries," he said to her. He thought about taking Duncan with him but decided it would give Mac-Lean more room in the car if he didn't.

"Will you tell my wife, Duncan . . .?"

Duncan nodded.

"Are there more trees down?" Cameron asked.

"Not this side of Shiel Bridge, Doctor," said one of the men. Cameron recognized the fellow as one of the gillies he'd encountered the day in early October, on the slopes of the Saddle.

The drive to Fort William would have been awkward even under good conditions. Cameron had to judge his speed and to position the car in relation to the road surface to minimize jolting. Whenever the car lurched at all appreciably, MacLean would cry out in distress. In the present high wind the drive was an abomination, particularly as Cameron had to stop repeatedly to deal with some form of obstacle. He could never get it out of his mind that sooner or later something across the road would prove beyond his strength to clear away. He kept cursing himself for coming without Duncan and he kept thinking it would have been better to have fastened MacLean in some way—so he wouldn't roll about so much.

It was with thankful relief that he turned the car into the hospital driveway. Two medical orderlies got MacLean out in expert style. Cameron marveled at the difference it made knowing exactly how to do a job, even an apparently simple job. He followed the orderlies into the hospital casualty section. A young house surgeon appeared and Cameron explained as best he could the circumstances of the accident. Then he turned to the injured man. "Ye'll be fine now, Tom. We'll be having ye back in no time at all. There'll be a powerful dram awaiting ye, man."

MacLean smiled weakly up at him.

The brief November afternoon was almost gone as Cameron began the return journey. On the outskirts of Fort William he decided to fill up the car, since there was no telling when petrol might run short in Glen Shiel. The evening air was sticky hot as he got out at one of the garages. "Can you fill right up?" he asked the attendant.

"Aye," said the fellow, unlocking the pumps. "I don't like this," he went on, looking up into the sky. "It's not right."

"There's nothing much that's right these days," agreed Cameron.

"Going toward Fort Augustus?"

"Aye."

"There was a girl through here about an hour ago. . . ."

"Walking?"

"No, but her car wouldn't get her far, I'm thinking."

Cameron paid for the petrol with a large note. The attendant handed him the change, saying, "She's a good-looking lass. You'll be spotting her easily enough."

Cameron drove north in the gathering dusk through Spean Bridge and up the long hill to the war memorial. Almost two miles beyond the side road to Gairloch he saw an old car at the roadside. Reckoning this might be the good-looking lass, he stopped. "In trouble?" he shouted.

"No, but I'm running out of ideas," came a female voice. A figure stepped out of the gloom to the side of Cameron's car. "I'd be grateful for a lift into Fort Augustus."

It had been Cameron's intention to turn at Invergarry for Glen Shiel, but he could easily go by the Invermoriston road.

"Get in," he said. "What's your name?"

"Janet," she said.

Cameron checked speed as soon as he reached the thick woods approaching Letterfindlay.

"On your way home?" he asked the girl.

"Yes, I was hoping to get there tonight, but it doesn't look like it now."

"You'll hardly get the car fixed until the morning."

"I know. I'll stay in Fort Augustus—there's a youth hostel."

"How far have you come?"

"Edinburgh—I'm a student there."

"University?"

"Yes, second year."

"How are things down in Edinburgh?"

"A lot of panic, if that's what you mean."

"At this galaxy thing?"

"Yes."

"I see; so you thought you'd come home."

"Yes."

Although they were in thick woods, and the sun had been set for almost an hour now, there was a glow of light everywhere, as if the moon were just risen. Cameron knew the thing must be appearing for a short time very low down in the southern sky. Yet he was unprepared for the auroral glow stretching entirely over the sky which became visible as soon as they quitted the woods a few miles before Invergarry. It stretched everywhere in vast tongues of flaming red. In the sticky heat it seemed as if they were imprisoned in a furnace of unlimited size.

Cameron knew what it was caused by—high-speed particles hitting the upper atmosphere. He knew it should be comparatively harmless but he kept wondering if his calculations could be wrong somewhere. Mistakes could be made, easily enough. He thought this girl ought to be getting home instead of fooling about with a decrepit car. "Where d'you live?" he asked.

"Near Cannich."

"I'll run you there," he said with sudden decision. He felt guilty in not having at least tried to get her car going again; but playing around with a strange car without proper light was always the devil.

"What's it all due to?" asked Janet softly.

"What are you studying—science?"

"No, history and philosophy and English." She went on, "What's going to happen?"

"Nobody knows yet."

"How bad is it going to be?"

"Fairly bad. Is your home old or new?"

"Old; it's a farmhouse."

"Good. Just sit tight when you get there."

"How long will it go on?"

"Not too long."

"How d'you mean?"

"Two or three weeks. A month maybe."

"That's not too long."

"No, you'll stick it out all right. Why didn't you go away with a boyfriend?"

"I don't have one, not that kind," answered the girl.

"Not strong enough?"

"No."

The storm which Cameron had feared broke north of Fort Augustus. Warm rain lashed the road ahead, glaring in the headlights of the car. The heavens too were alight. This was ordinary lightning now but it had an altogether extraordinary intensity. Cameron knew it to be caused by a devastating mixture of hot humid air from the south with cold air from the north. It was impossible to maintain any speed. The road to the Drumnadrochit turn for Cannich seemed endless, to such a degree that Cameron felt himself condemned to drive on and on throughout eternity.

There were obstacles on the Cannich road, stones and tree branches, mostly branches. Each time they had to stop and clear the route. Soon they were soaked. When they reached Cannich village the girl leaned over and said, "Take the road to the right." This was the Struy road. Only a month ago Cameron and Madeleine had come this way. With a sense of presentiment, Cameron asked above the wind, "Where exactly do you live?"

"Strathfarrar."

It was absurd to be still thinking of retribution for his dog, but the thought was in Cameron's mind as he brought the car to a stop before the same gate which had stopped him before.

"It'll be locked. I'll get it opened," the girl shouted.

She forced the car door open. Cameron watched her leaning into the rain as she staggered toward the cottage on the left. There was inevitable delay but eventually the gate was opened. Cameron guessed the woman holding it against the wind would be the same old woman who had stopped him before. Then the girl was back in the car. "Mrs. MacCrea will leave it unlocked. So you can get out again. God, it's wild," she said.

Once again the narrow strip of road heading westward up the glen seemed to continue for an eternity, an eternity of hairtrigger attention for Cameron. In this blinding storm it was almost like driving in a thick fog. At last Janet reached over, putting a hand on his arm. "There's a place where you can turn just ahead."

He found the place and stopped. The girl made no move to get out, so he switched off the engine.

"It's going to be bad, isn't it?" she whispered tensely.

Cameron hesitated, and she went on, "I'm going to die. We're all going to die." The grip on his arm tightened convulsively.

"I wouldn't . . ." he began.

His emotions raced away with him. He took firm hold of the girl and helped her into the back of the vehicle.

"I must go," she gasped at length, straightening her clothes. Cameron made a half-hearted attempt to stop her but she pushed him away.

"No, no. I must go," she said. Cameron knew that any superficial aspects of the permissive society which she might have acquired in her two years at Edinburgh had fallen from her. She was once again the apprehensive Highland girl, apprehensive of men, apprehensive of the world. He let her go without further demonstration.

He drove back to the gate by Struy. It was unlocked, so he didn't trouble to get the old woman out of her cottage. The wind tore at the gate as he swung it open. On sudden impulse he loosed it into the gale. It swung back, gaining furious speed, and crashed violently against the upright post. Well aware of the bursting strain on the hinges, Cameron repeated the process again and yet again. On the third try, the gate cracked and splintered. But it was jammed tightly at both ends, although broken quite badly near the hinges. Finding he couldn't shift it by hand now, he got back into the Rover, engaged the low gears, selected first, edged against the gate, raced the engine and let the clutch in gently. The vehicle pushed firmly forward, tearing the gate apart. Cameron left it strewn across the road. He doubted the way up to Strathfarrar would ever be closed again.

It was near midnight by the time Cameron reached Glen Shiel again. The hardest decision was not to take the shortcut up Glen Moriston. He decided it was best to keep to roads which he knew to be open. This meant crawling back through Fort Augustus to Invergarry. On the top above Cluanie there were moments when it seemed that even the heavy Range Rover might be blown off the road. It was necessary to drive at a snail's pace most of the way.

Cameron stopped at Duncan Fraser's cottage. He told him Tom MacLean was fine in hospital and asked him to drop the word to Mrs. MacLean. Then with apprehension for the safety of his own house he drove the final two miles, to find Madeleine waiting up for him. He barely had time to strip and rub down before she had hot food ready. He ate avidly. He had not realized how very hungry he had become. Then at last he was into bed, but not yet to sleep. Madeleine came immediately to him, her mouth more urgent than he remembered it.

"I thought something must have happened," she whispered.

Without remorse he pulled her to him.

Cameron slept late in spite of the heat, which was becoming worse hour by hour. After breakfast he went back to the donkey engine. There was still no main electric supply, and not likely to be. The donkey engine would obviate the need for candles, which Madeleine had used the previous evening. At least it was something to be done. He was making what he hoped would be final adjustments when a Land Rover bounced to a stop on the roadway by the side of the house. Thinking it would be Duncan Fraser, come to ask for more details about Tom Mac-Lean, Cameron wiped his hands on a cloth and began walking toward the vehicle.

It was Duncan all right, but with him were two men, both young fellows, both with gum boots, rough slacks, sweaters and woolen caps.

"This is Hamish Chisholm," said Duncan, pointing to the shorter of the two. Hamish was very broad of shoulder, blue-eyed with fair complexion, and with a big beard.

"And this is Toddy MacKenzie," concluded Duncan. Mac-Kenzie was a big chap, not much shorter than Cameron himself, and like Cameron he was clean shaven.

"We came to see you, Dr. Cameron, on behalf of the local crofters," explained Chisholm.

Cameron held up his oil-stained hand. "I'll not be shaking hands," he said. "You'd best be coming inside."

Madeleine brought them coffee.

"What's to be done, that's what we want to know," began Chisholm.

"Let me get it straight," Cameron answered. "You've got an association of crofters—I've heard about it before." Mac-Kenzie and Chisholm nodded. "How many are there—I mean how far does the association go?"

"We've got affiliations through the county. But . . ."

"That's what I wanted to know. So you could get a fair bit of action, if you had to."

"That's right, Dr. Cameron. But what kind of action? That's what we want to know," Chisholm said again.

"Let's be clear from the beginning: this is a bad situation."

"Aye, it's bad away to the south all right," agreed Mac-Kenzie.

"They seem to be after getting the government out of London," interposed Duncan.

"You heard it on the news?" asked Cameron.

"Aye." Duncan infused the single syllable with a grim finality.

"Well, you'll be wanting to make sure everybody is properly sheltered."

"We've started that already, Dr. Cameron," said Chisholm.

"Let's set down the things to be done." Cameron took a sheet of paper and wrote out a list:

1. Shelter
2. Food and Fuel
3. Animals
4. Boats
5. Guns
6. Motors and Engines
7. Seeds

"I'm writing these things down just as they occur to me—not necessarily in order of priority," he explained.

"You make it sound like a siege, Dr. Cameron," exclaimed Chisholm.

"If you weren't thinking the same you wouldn't have come along here, would you?"

"That's true too," admitted MacKenzie, sucking in air. *"I'm not liking the day,"* he added.

"And tomorrow liking it still less," observed Cameron.

"Ah, you have the Gaelic, Doctor!"

"Aye, and I'm thinking we may yet be speaking it again."

"What would you be meaning by that, Doctor?" Chisholm asked. Cameron stood up, paced to the big window facing onto the loch. "It'll be many a day before you see any landlords from the south again," he said decisively.

"Would that be the idea of the guns, Doctor?" MacKenzie had risen now.

"At the end of this thing, if we're still alive at its end, we shall only keep what we can hold. Let that be known to every man around this loch. I see a great wave of people from the south, I see waves coming at us through every valley from Inverness down to Fort William."

There was a long silence as the crofters adjusted themselves to Cameron's statement.

"How about cars, Dr. Cameron? You haven't said anything about cars and lorries." Chisholm's bushy eyebrows were raised high.

"Keep your precious cars, if you must," grunted Cameron, "but how long d'you think you'll be able to use 'em?"

"You mean petrol?"

"Of course."

"There'll be a fair amount of petrol and oil in Kyle."

"It would be best not to use it except in emergencies. The Strome ferry is more important. Without Strome ferry there'll be no way to the north."

"The new road—"

"The Attadale road will become impassable. It's probably blocked already," said Cameron, peering out the window.

"Aye, we always said it was in a bad place," agreed MacKenzie.

"But the county council wouldn't hear anything about it," added Duncan.

"A lot of know-nothings from Inverness," said Chisholm with warmth, his beard rising and falling.

MacKenzie began slowly to roll a cigarette. "Do you mind, Doctor?" he asked.

"No, go ahead."

"What you're telling us, Doctor," MacKenzie went on, "is that we're on our own. Would that be it now?"

"I'm telling you to prepare for it that way."

"Aye, I can see the sense of that. To prepare for the worst."

Cameron forbore to tell MacKenzie that it was for the best he was advising them to prepare. The worst would be beyond their imagination.

He saw the three outside to the Land Rover. They drove away, Duncan at the wheel, MacKenzie puffing his rolled cigarette, sweat pouring down their faces. Cameron returned yet again to the donkey engine. He swung it and the thing started. He began checking the voltages when he heard Madeleine shout. "Not again," he muttered to himself, going out of the little shed to join his wife, wondering what the devil it would be this time.

He found her in the garden at the back of the house. "Just look at those roses," she shouted. "Practically a flower show."

Cameron could see the heat was bringing out the spring flowers. He could see crocuses pushing upward from their winter retreat. Madeleine began picking the roses. "When will the time come?" she asked suddenly.

"What time?" asked Cameron stupidly.

"When we're going to die. That's what's happening in other places. It's only a question of time, isn't it? Like *On the Beach*?"

"I don't know."

"You do, of course you do. I can see it in your face. You won't let me die painfully, will you? I've got two bottles of sleeping pills."

Cameron put his arm around her shoulders. "Look, I wouldn't be fixing that old engine if I thought it was as bad as that, would I? Suppose you make a bit of lunch."

Madeleine went back to the house, thinking that fixing the old engine would be exactly what her husband would do, even if Death himself were walking up the road. She did her best to get it out of her head, but the morning news kept reasserting itself in her mind. She thought of switching on the battery radio again but decided against it. She felt hot and clammy and went to take a bath.

Cameron decided to try the automatic starter. He pressed a switch and the engine rumbled into life, sending a cloud of black smoke out of the exhaust. Then he cut the switch and went to check that the piping up to the roof was still in place. He fitted a garden spray to the end of the pipe, climbed down from the roof and turned on the water in the kitchen. The spray should cool things a bit, although the air was very humid. Madeleine was out of the bathroom now, so he cleaned himself of the engine dirt and grease, and sat down to a salad lunch. He thought he would spend the afternoon seeing if he could use the electric supply from the engine to operate the deep-freeze unit.

The afternoon was dark. Heavy clouds made for a murky gloom already by two o'clock. Cameron walked to the lochside. He'd got a notion the water level might have risen slightly. If the polar ice caps were to melt in this great heat most of the houses around the lochside would be inundated. This was another possible cause of disaster. He thought he'd better check up on the energy requirements. An eerie light was spreading across the sky now. Another monstrous storm was on its way. Cameron hoped he wouldn't have to turn out with his car again that night. He went inside and soon checked that the polar ice caps wouldn't melt, not sufficiently to produce much lifting of the sea level anyway.

The storm broke. For a while Cameron found himself unable to sit still. Restlessly he switched on the donkey engine again. It worked, so he switched it off. He checked the pipe to the roof. He padded in the gloom backward and forward in front of the big window. He tried the battery radio but either because of heavy static, or because the BBC really was off the air, he failed to raise anything. Then he slumped in a chair and simply watched the storm. Suddenly he was aware of a diffuse light on the far side of the loch and knew it for fire caused by a lightning strike. And all the while it seemed to be getting hotter and hotter.

During the next three days of increasing heat mildew grew everywhere. A sickly sweet smell settled over the house. Cameron didn't dare to switch on the engine now, because the insulation would be quite inadequate. So he and Madeleine were in darkness or in semidarkness all the time, in semidarkness even during the few hours when the sun was up, because of heavy low clouds.

Cameron and Madeleine lay helpless in delirium. Cameron had realized at an earlier stage that, while his dramatic prognostication of a total uplift of the earth's atmosphere would be correct ultimately, they were to die quite undramatically. The temperature had risen above body heat. With humidity of 100 percent, death by heat prostration was not far away. To begin with he'd regretted not equipping himself with a simple thermometer. Now the delirium was on him, the torment in his disordered mind was that if only he could somehow determine his body temperature everything would be resolved. He lay there, his heart thumping loudly in his ears. The upper register was gone now. There was just a hollow base throbbing. Madeleine fought her way through a deep impenetrable jungle toward the sleeping pills which she knew would resolve everything. She fought desperately to reach for them but all she could manage was a feeble flapping of the hand.

Everything was quite black now. Not even at midday was there a glimmer of light.

This was in latitude fifty-seven degrees north, a latitude favored by winter conditions and by the circumstance that it was almost completely turned away from the hellish thing at the center of the galaxy. At Mount Bogung Observatory the thing had been riding through the zenith for some days now, a blazing point of light of overwhelming intensity. Temperatures had risen throughout the equatorial and subtropical zones of the earth, far above anything at which life could be supported. In the developed countries people remained alive in places where communal power supplies were still operative through the help of air-conditioning equipment. Yet few such people had escaped the deadly radiation which now poured through the atmosphere with an intensity many thousands of times above the maximum dosage which can be accepted by humans and others of the higher animals. Governments in a number of countries managed to retreat underground, where they too remained operative thanks to air-conditioning equipment. Of all people the Eskimos of the far north were most favorably placed. Yet even the Eskimos found themselves seriously affected by the untimely melting of rivers and snow fields which cut them off from their traditional routes and from most of their normal food supplies. The pulse of life on the earth was now beating low. Worst affected were the creatures of the air, least affected the creatures of the sea.

The hours dragged by in total blackness. Slowly, over several days, the temperature fell, degree by degree. As the temperature fell, the fever which tormented Cameron's brain became less and less acute. His mind retreated from blackness by the way it had come, first through a frenzied search for the elusive thermometer, then to the conscious realization of the fever in his brain, then to coherent thought—suddenly, as if a mental switch had been pressed. He was afraid now for Madeleine, until he had checked that her heart was still beating. He searched blindly around for the two bottles of sleeping pills. When he found them he threw both across the room and sank back exhausted.

After what he knew to be a long gap Cameron was awake again, feeling a great deal better now. Rain was falling heavily outside. It was still totally dark. He wondered again about starting the donkey engine but knew the insulation just wouldn't stand it. The bedclothes were wet and horrible. He shook Madeleine until she was awake, still fearful she might have overdosed herself with the pills.

"Where are we?" she whispered eventually.

"Home."

"We're not dead."

"No, we're not dead."

"Why is it so dark?"

"I don't know."

"What's wrong with the bed?"

"Everything's soaked."

"Is it raining in?"

"I'm not sure, but I think it must be sweat and condensation."

"We ought to change everything."

So Cameron stumbled about the house until he found an electric torch. Madeleine used the torch to find the candles and now at least they had light. Everything in the house was damp but at least damp new bedclothes and pajamas were better than the old things. Madeleine tried to make a warm drink but the gas wasn't working. Guessing the pilot light must have gone out, Cameron relit it without difficulty. Fearful of a gas leak, he decided to check the piping all the way from the house to the big cylinder outside. He found the rain now torrential. Then they were back in bed, drinking hot cocoa with milk made from powder. Within minutes they were both asleep again.

The rain was beating like continuous thunder when Cameron next awoke. For some reason the temperature outside must be falling. The hot air must have become charged with an enormous quantity of water vapor, which was falling as rain, now the air was becoming cooler. This made sense.

It was still totally black outside. He had an urge to find out the time of day, but all three watches in the house were stopped. He restarted his own watch, setting it arbitrarily at twelve o'clock. He made toast and a pot of tea. After eating the toast he found Madeleine awake, so he boiled a couple of eggs for her. The rain outside seemed to have moderated somewhat but it was still heavy. Cameron racked his brains to think what he should be doing next but finding nothing urgent he went back to bed. Sleep came again. It was approaching six o'clock on his watch. When he awoke the rain was definitely less heavy than it had been.

The hours passed and it was still totally dark.

"Why is it so dark?" Madeleine kept asking.

Cameron simply answered that he didn't know, and in truth he had to admit to himself that he really didn't. By now he'd followed his watch almost through a whole day, and there was still no sign of daylight.

Although the temperature fell imperceptibly, degree by degree, there came a definite moment, quite sharply, when Cameron and Madeleine were aware of a new regime. Instead of being hot they were suddenly chilly. This was easily dealt with by starting up the central heating, which gradually dried away the damp in the house. The clammy sweet smell was less strong now.

The rain had stopped. Lying in bed they could hear the nearby stream raging in the blackness outside. Cameron wondered why he hadn't worried himself about the stream bursting its banks, about it flooding the house and perhaps sweeping the house into the loch. But it was too late to bother himself about that now. Luckily the stream was on a fair slope. It must simply have increased its speed to cope with the extra water—which was why it was thundering so loudly.

The temperature continued to fall. Cameron put on his mountaineering clothes and made a trip outside to check on the gas supply. He knew the cylinder to which they were connected must be running low. He decided to switch the supply to one of the new cylinders delivered recently from Inverness.

With this done he stood staring up into a totally black sky. He was surprised there were no stars, because the air couldn't be holding much water now. Once again he wished he'd had the foresight to equip himself with a thermometer. Suddenly it flashed into his mind that it would be good to drain the car. With the car new, and him not knowing the layout of the engine, it was some time before he found the drain cock. By now his hands were desperately cold. Cameron was heartily thankful to rush back inside the house as soon as the job was done.

As the temperature fell it was at first quite pleasant, clad only in pajamas, in the centrally heated house. Then they took to remaining fully dressed, even in bed. Cameron was lying on the bed puzzling about the long continued blackness, when there came a furious knocking. He had come to think of Madeleine and himself as the only two living creatures left on the earth. Almost in panic, he reached for the electric torch as the knocking continued. Opening the door and flashing the now waning torch, he saw it was Duncan Fraser.

"It's cold, Doctor," whispered Duncan.

"Come inside."

Fraser stumbled across the doorstep and Cameron slammed the outer door.

"What is it?" continued Cameron.

"The cold, Dr. Cameron. It's getting too cold, especially for the old people."

Cameron realized how appallingly cold it must be in the old stone houses. "Can you get them here?" he asked.

"That's what I was wondering. . . . Are you sure you wouldn't mind, Doctor?"

"Can they walk?"

"Not everybody."

"Is the Land Rover running?"

"I can't start it. The oil is too thick."

"Get everybody here who can walk, Duncan. I'll work on my car and see if I can get it started."

Madeleine had appeared. "Where shall we put them all?" she asked as soon as Duncan had gone.

"Those who are sick get the beds. The rest of us have the floor," grunted Cameron.

"How about food?"

"It's lucky we laid in a good stock, isn't it?"

The drain cock on the car was frozen, so Cameron took hot water from the house and poured it into the engine. Eventually water began oozing through the cock and at last he was able to close it. The car swallowed up a second and a third pail of hot water. The water was now freezing on his hands so he went indoors again and waited. Duncan was a long time, so Cameron went back to the car. The hot water had helped to reduce the viscosity of the cold engine oil and he was able to start it after two or three attempts.

Duncan appeared at last with perhaps a dozen folk. They stumbled across the doorstep into the warmth of the house. Madeleine had hot tea ready for them. Then Duncan and Cameron went out to the car.

"The road is bad, with ice everywhere, Doctor."

Very slowly they drove into Letterfearn. Twice the wheels began to spin, in spite of the four-wheel, low-geared drive, but each time they eventually found enough purchase to enable the car to crawl forward.

Duncan knew the houses where help had been needed. But for all except the last, help had come too late. The appalling heat and the desperate cold had been too much for the older people. At the last house Cameron was astonished to hear the yell of a baby.

"Kathy MacIver's baby was born during the rain," explained Duncan.

"Without a doctor?" asked Cameron foolishly.

"There was a nurse—Mrs. MacDonald."

"Where's Mrs. MacDonald?"

"She was in one of the houses we just visited."

Cameron sucked in his breath.

They bundled the baby with as much clothing as they could reasonably get around its small body. Duncan carried it to the car. Cameron followed with Kathy MacIver. He wrapped the woman in his thermal jacket. The way back through the ice was no easier than before. Every few yards there was danger of sliding. Cameron and Fraser could walk. So probably could Kathy MacIver, but her baby would not survive if the car should come off the road.

Duncan asked him to stop. Thinking there might be trouble ahead, Cameron checked speed too quickly, getting into a skid which he just managed to hold.

"There are some things over by the house," said Duncan.

Cameron got out in a fury, walked to the door of the house and in the light from the car saw a collection of kerosene lamps and a five-gallon drum. He put the lamps in the back of the car and then called to Duncan.

"You'd better give me a hand with the kerosene."

Fraser climbed across the driver's seat. He shivered as he walked to join Cameron by the house. Together they carried the drum to the car. Cameron was still angry when they started again. He found it better than his former apprehension. At all events he found less difficulty with the last part of the journey. Arriving at his home, he helped Kathy MacIver and her baby inside, recovered his jacket from the girl, and went outside yet again to help Duncan with the kerosene, and to drain the car. To do Duncan justice, they would have lights now, but it would have been better to have brought the baby first and then to have fetched the lamps in a separate journey. Cameron was acutely conscious of the need to make even small decisions correctly now. In the old life small mistakes, like a car off the road, had been punished only by inconvenience. In the future, if there was a future, small mistakes could lead to disaster. It was for this reason he'd made Duncan help him with the kerosene drum. Cameron wasn't risking a slipped disk, because injuries, even simple ones, could mean death now.

He was angry again to find that nothing sensible had been done for the several people, mostly the older ones, who were suffering from exposure. He told them, with a force not to be denied, to get into a hot bath instead of huddling in a chair or on the floor. When he had stirred them into action he left Madeleine to find drying materials—towels, curtains, what did it matter—and took himself off with one of the lamps into a little study. His problem was to think ahead to the next possible difficulty. If the outside temperature continued ever downward, sooner or later the liquid gas would freeze and their heat would be gone. Cameron looked up in a chemical handbook the freezing temperature of butane. He found it to be very low, so low that the first trouble would come from defective insulation of the house, not from the gas supply. Since he couldn't start rebuilding the house there was nothing to be done about that. He kept pondering the reason for the continued blackness. It almost seemed as if the earth had been blown away from the sun, but that surely was impossible. Besides, the stars should then be visible, which they weren't.

A vague light spread gradually across the eastern sky, the light of a late November morning. It was five days since the people from Letterfearn had taken refuge at Cameron's house, five days in which he had frequently expressed the hope—to himself—that he would never again be compelled to listen at close range to a screaming baby.

The light had not long come to Glen Shiel when Cameron stepped outside into the bitter air. He walked to the lochside, his boots squeaking in very dry snow. The sight which met his eyes as he gazed up the glen was appalling beyond all expectations. So it must have been during the Ice Age. The Five Sisters range was plastered, bottom to top, with ice and snow. So were Beinn Fhada and the mountains north of Morvich. The loch itself was thick frozen. It was a white world of intense desolation. It was the white of a shroud. Cameron found himself scarely able to believe that the land it covered could ever come to life again.

10

The Aftermath

The temperature rose gradually day by day but it was still far too low for there to be any melting of the snow or of the loch. Daylight came and went normally now. The little community on the south side of the loch had ample fuel and food for its immediate needs. But straightaway there were problems which Cameron hadn't anticipated. Duncan Fraser came to him. "We ought to be after burying the dead, Doctor," he said, scratching his head underneath his deerstalker hat. "But the ground is as hard as a stone."

The solution occurred to Cameron almost immediately. In the cold the bodies would not decay at all appreciably, but to leave them in the houses was not to be thought of. Nor was it right for the morale of the community simply to place them on the ground outside.

"You've got ample wood, Duncan. Burn the corpses."

Cameron's voice was firm and decisive. He knew he would need to be sharp and clear on this thing, to overcome ingrained prejudices about the kind of treatment which was right and proper for the dead.

They obeyed his instructions to build a funeral pyre but they did so in a sullen manner. He made them place the bodies on the stacked wood. Then he spoke to the little community in Gaelic. He spoke well for he remembered the priest's speech from *Peer Gynt* and he knew that to speak in such a style was better than a formal prayer. Then he made them put fire to the wood. When the flames had risen high he took Duncan Fraser on one side.

"Ye see now, Duncan, why it was necessary for the Vikings to burn their dead."

Fraser stared at him for a moment and then said, "Aye, Doctor, but they were a heathen folk."

Cameron decided that henceforth he was giving no more gratuitous explanations.

Eilean Donan Castle had collapsed. Cameron thought about walking across the loch to Dornie. The ice was firm enough at the lochside but he suspected there would be leads toward the middle, caused by warmer water stirred up from below. He decided the risk would be foolish.

Two days later Hamish Chisholm and two other men appeared at the house. "We saw your fire," explained Chisholm. Then he introduced Willy MacDonald and Tom Murray, assuring Cameron they were powerful men with boats.

"We're not doing much with boats till the loch melts," said Cameron.

"Aye," agreed MacDonald. He was a small, wiry middleaged man, the kind to have survived through the past weeks. Murray nodded and sucked hard on an empty pipe.

"Ye'll best be coming inside out of the cold," said Cameron. "And how about MacKenzie?"

"He was away over to the Glenelg side."

"You've had it pretty comfortable, Cameron," said Chisholm when they were inside.

"We were lucky, being sheltered on this side of the loch. Otherwise this house would have been down."

"Aye," said MacDonald, still wearing his woolly cap. Cameron guessed he wore it all the time, indoors as well as out, just as Tom Murray seemed to chew his pipe the whole time.

"Did ye walk?" asked Cameron.

"The last part. There's no way through to Shiel Bridge on this side," answered Chisholm. The man had lost a lot of weight and there was a telling strain in his eyes, which seemed more sharply blue than before. "We got a Land Rover through on the other side, with a bit of trouble. Cracked cylinder block," he added.

Cameron grinned wryly. "There can't be many vehicles without cracked engines, I've been thinking. I've got one of 'em out there but we can't get it through to Shiel. Not for a while anyway."

Madeleine brought in some coffee. Chisholm jumped up to help her with the tray. Then he turned to Cameron. "You seem always to be thinking ahead—I reckon that's why we came."

"I've been thinking Dornie would be the best center," began Cameron.

"It's not as comfortable as this."

"No, but this place is hopeless as a communications center. What's still usable in Dornie?"

"In the village itself, some of the houses. We've got people in the Ardelve Hotel."

"The schoolhouse?"

"Still standing," interposed Murray.

"Could it be used?"

"I suppose so," said Chisholm.

"Let's plan it this way, Chisholm. I want the schoolroom tidied up. I want you to meet me at Shiel two days from now, as close on midday as you can make it."

"Ye've got a plan, Doctor?" asked MacDonald.

"Aye, I've a plan all right, but I'm not talking about it today. Get me ten of the best men you can find. Get them to the schoolhouse. I want the schoolmaster and I want the doctor."

Chisholm stirred his coffee. "If you can see what is to be done, Cameron, we'll follow you," he said simply.

Because he was no longer offering explanations, Cameron

didn't trouble to tell them that he had been looking to this day for a long time now, more or less since he had left Australia. Everything had fallen gradually into place.

Madeleine was not keen to quit her house, so Cameron simply gave her the alternatives of staying there or of coming with him to Dornie. Faced with the choice, she elected to go to Dornie. Two days later she and Cameron walked the five miles from Letterfearn to Shiel Bridge. Madeleine sensed that she was on the edge of a new life, a life to which she was not well suited. During the walk through the frozen wilderness she was closer psychologically to her husband than she would be again for many a long month.

Hamish Chisholm was waiting at Shiel. It took an hour and a half to thread their way the ten miles to Dornie. Three times Cameron and Chisholm had to refill the cracked Land Rover engine with water, which they did from cans, the streams along the roadside being frozen. They left Madeleine at the Ardelve Hotel. Cameron saw the forlorn look on her face as the Land Rover pulled away. It would have been better for her to have stayed at Letterfearn, he thought.

There were close on twenty men assembled in the schoolroom. Chisholm recited their names. Oddly enough, Cameron knew he wouldn't forget them, presumably because now it really mattered that he should know them all. He was glad to see Toddy MacKenzie back from the Glenelg side. Toddy gave him a nod in place of an introduction and continued rolling a cigarette. Cameron dumped a rucksack which he'd brought on the front desk and sat down facing the men. He thought of speaking in Gaelic but decided one or two mightn't understand him any too well, which would be an embarrassment. So he began, "Dr. Nicolson, you've got first priority. I'm going to ask you to organize the medical side."

"I've been thinking about that, especially about how we're going to get people over to Fort William."

"It's going to be a long long day before you send another

patient to Fort William," Cameron stated in a flat, strong voice. "You're thrown back on your own resources now."

"But for years we've depended on sending serious cases away. . . ."

"I know. So you haven't got too much in the way of resources —which is exactly why I'm giving you first priority. That's on the debit side. On the credit side, you're going to find more strength than maybe you expect. I mean doctors who were working in the south who came home when things became bad. I don't think you'll be thrown back on yourself and maybe a doctor in Kyle. I think you'll get a fair group together. Which is just the first thing to be done. Find out what doctors there are. Go as far up and down the coast as you can. Get out a list of trained nurses."

"That'll be all right." Nicolson nodded.

"You mean there are a good number—of nurses?"

"I'm sure of it."

"Next, when you've got the shape of it, get the doctors together and some of the nurses. Find out exactly what medical stores you've got."

"That might involve quite a bit of foraging."

"It might, and I'll suggest you approach Hamish Chisholm here for any help you need. Hamish, I'm charging you to give Dr. Nicolson whatever material help he might need—as a first priority."

Chisholm nodded. Sensing a relaxation in the men, Cameron knew he was adopting the right tone.

"Next, Mr. Hamilton." The schoolmaster, Hamilton, was surprised to hear his name mentioned so soon. "Mr. Hamilton, I've brought this for you. You'd better examine it." Cameron pointed to the rucksack. Hamilton came forward rather awkwardly and opened up the rucksack. He fumbled around inside it for a moment and then drew out an ordnance map. There were wide grins around the room.

"Those maps are without price, Mr. Hamilton. Maybe in a shop here and there you'll find one or two local maps, but these give a full coverage of the whole Highlands. What I want you to do, Mr. Hamilton, is to compile a list, a big list, of all the people—all the farms."

"You mean a sort of *Doomsday Book?*" asked Hamilton, grasping the point very quickly.

"That's exactly what I mean. This is a matter of extreme urgency. Until we've got your book, Mr. Hamilton, we can't know exactly what our total resources are, and we can't know what our responsibilities are either. Recruit all the help you need. You know the right people for this job much better than I do."

Hamilton nodded.

"Yes, and another thing," added Cameron. "Aim toward a library. We're going to need all manner of simple manuals. Unless someone is responsible they'll soon get scattered and lost. The same thing for cultural books generally. You understand?"

"Of course," said Hamilton, half smiling now.

"Third, Sergeant Forsythe," went on Cameron, nodding toward a man dressed in a tattered police uniform. "Sergeant, ye'll know better than any of us here the need for law and order, the need for clear rules, if people are to live and work together."

"But what is the law, Mr. Cameron, that's what I've been asking myself these past days."

"Ye'll not have been receiving instructions?"

"Not a word."

"Well, Sergeant, it isn't just a matter of a few telephone wires being blown down. Ye'll have listened to the radio."

"That's just the trouble," exclaimed Forsythe. "The radio is one big nothing."

"So ye'll have been wondering what manner of law it is which is to be applied in this land?"

"Aye, I've been wondering."

"There'll be no closing hours, I'm telling ye that, man," said Tom Murray, still biting his empty pipe.

"*I* am telling *you* what the law is, Sergeant," said Cameron in full voice. "As long as all our lives are under threat there will be no personal property—no houses, no boats, no animals, no fuel, no food. . . . All these things will belong to the community."

"And how about the clothes I'm wearing, Doctor?" came a voice.

Cameron grinned but there was no humor in his face. "Aye," he said, "and using a bit of common sense—that'll be the second law."

"It's asking a lot," muttered Chisholm.

"So Hamish, you've got a nice bit of seed in store—maybe because I told you to get it. You'll be planting a potato patch in a few months, supposing you're lucky and the snows melt. Sometime in the summer you'll be harvesting those potatoes— if you're still lucky." Cameron wagged his finger at Chisholm. "By then, Hamish, you're going to be mighty hungry. More likely you'll be eating all that seed, and then maybe none of us here will ever see a fresh potato again."

Cameron stood up and his eyes swept over the room, dominating them with his height and with the strength of his personality. "There are men here with boats," he went on. "They will catch fish when the ice melts. There are men with shops in Kyle with stores of food, who can eat now, but who will inevitably starve when their stocks become exhausted. Somewhere among you there may be a few men with everything—stocks of food, boats, animals, potato seed. But let me tell you this: Such a lucky man will keep neither his food, nor his boat, nor his animals, nor his seed, without the protection of Sergeant Forsythe."

Forsythe nodded. "The Cameron is right," he said with total conviction.

This was the first time the ancient title had been used. Cameron swept on. "For the moment we are all much luckier than any of you yet realizes. For the moment we've got stocks of food, clothing and fuel. These stocks are never going to be replaced. Understand that gentlemen—*never.*"

Chisholm was nodding now. "So we must use these things to get started," he said.

"Right," boomed Cameron, "to get started. There will be no second chance." He turned again to the policeman.

"Sergeant Forsythe, you are to be our quartermaster. All material stores are your responsibility."

"Petrol as well as food?"

"Yes."

"And where does the ultimate authority lie?"

"It lies with *me*," growled Cameron.

Forsythe nodded. "I know my rules now."

Cameron turned back to Hamish Chisholm.

"And now I come to you farmers and crofters. What is the animal situation, cows and sheep and hens?"

"Bad," grunted Chisholm. "A cow here and there and a few sheep."

"Collect all sheep into a flock. The ice near the shoreline will be the first to melt. The sheep can live for a while on the seaweed."

"And the cows?"

"There won't be natural grazing for months yet. If there's adequate fodder where the cows are now, leave 'em. Otherwise move the beasts to where there's fodder—or the other way round."

"We draw petrol for this?"

"For moving fodder, yes. For collecting animals, not unless there's urgency."

"What is urgent?"

"Whether the animal lives or dies."

145

Cameron then turned to MacKenzie. "You're been away over to Glenelg?"

"Aye."

Cameron judged MacKenzie to be more a nomad than a farmer. "Toddy, I'm wanting a watch kept on the road above Cluanie. I'm betting it's badly flooded at the moment. But sooner or later we shall be getting strangers coming through."

"Ye'll be wanting them stopped, Mr. Cameron?"

"If they come in ones and twos, and if they're our own kind —no. If they come in bands—yes."

"And how am I to stop a band of men, now?"

"With men of your own. How else?"

"With the guns?"

"Aye, with the guns."

Toddy stood there, a half-smoked cigarette stuck in the corner of his mouth. He moved his cloth cap from the back of his head to the front. "I'm understanding ye, Mr. Cameron."

A voice spoke up from the back. "Mr. Cameron, I'm a post office engineer. Name of Halliday, Jim Halliday. I'm not a native of these parts. I happened to be up here on a job."

"Aye?"

"Mr. Chisholm there asked me about getting together a collection of electric motors."

"Ah, I'm glad of that, Mr. Halliday. Maybe ye'll have a word with me at the end."

Cameron knew he'd carried the meeting. There was no point in prolonging it. And several of the men were obviously itching to get started, so he stood and gave Halliday a signal. The man came forward.

"Those electric motors, Mr. Halliday."

"Yes, I've got a good dozen quite decent jobs."

"Ye'd best walk the road with me. I want to go to the Ardelve Hotel."

Outside on the road, Cameron swept his arm around the loch. "You can see the communication problem," he began.

"We don't have enough men and equipment to restart the telephones."

"No, but I've been reckoning we can go a long way with simple walkie-talkies. If we can find enough of them. With luck we might scrape together a dozen sets."

"And use them from strategic points?"

"In the short term we can operate 'em with batteries," continued Cameron. "In the long term we'll run out of batteries and out of generator fuel. In the long term we'll have to think of wind generators."

"Windmills? To small dynamos?"

"Which we'll get from the cars," concluded Cameron.

"It'll make a hell of a difference to the communal organization."

"You can do it? Technically I mean."

"Of course. It's right in my line."

"Then see Sergeant Forsythe. Tell him what you need."

Madeleine was waiting at the hotel. "It's a pig sty," she exclaimed passionately to Cameron.

"Like enough. Why not change it?" he replied.

They looked at each other for a long time, both wondering what had happened, and both thinking the other somewhat deranged.

11

The World Outside

The weeks and months passed inexorably away. Events followed in a rigorously logical order. The sea melted gradually. With the coming of spring and early summer the snow line retreated up the mountainsides, with great quantities of snow and ice still remaining on the high ridges. Grass appeared on the low ground. Flowers were there too, at first tentatively but then with the coming of May in an almost normal profusion. Yet nowhere could any birds be found. Indigenous birds had not survived and there were no migratory birds.

The community which Cameron had established from Kintail to Kyle grew with an equally rigorous logic. His almost instantaneous mobilization of the slender resources of the district gave it a coherence and strength which less organized small communities of survivors on the west coast of the Highlands could not match. The effect was to produce a quickly spreading influence of the Kintail-Kyle community. To the immediate south there was but Glenelg and scattered crofts from Glenelg to Arnisdale. These were helped from the beginning. With fuel from Kyle, a ferry was kept running at Strome. This soon brought the whole Lochcarron valley into the tightly knit organization, which then spread through Achnasheen to the west. Within six months, communication had become estab-

lished from Gairloch in the north to Mallaig in the south, and
ferries were beginning to connect Skye to the mainland again.

Cameron knew from the beginning the way things must go
logistically. He also knew that a changed way of life would not
come to the western Highlands without sharp human incidents,
of a kind that wouldn't be quelled by the simple appearance of
Sergeant Forsythe's tattered police uniform. Cameron had no
established laws and precedents to fall back on. Each outbreak
would have to be dealt with on its own merits. Dealt with and
finished with, whatever the cost.

Sometimes incidents turned out better than might have been
expected, sometimes worse. There seemed to be no predicting
the way things would go from a human point of view. An
incident occurred at a farm near Quoich Bridge which started
badly and ended well. A young man from one of Toddy Mac-
Kenzie's patrols was shot dead while trying to approach the
farm. His two companions retreated in the face of accurate
rifle fire directed from the farm buildings. Cameron himself
took a strong party across the Bealach Duibh. He went in anger,
knowing this particular farm to have been owned by an Englishman. The Englishman had made something of a reputation
from breeding Highland cattle of the old kind, perversely
enough. Cameron took his party into the farm after nightfall. It
needed no great measure of tactical skill for them to arrive without sound at the very doorstep of the farmhouse itself. While
one group of men battered directly and obviously on the main
door, others broke stealthily through the windows. Within
minutes they had the farmer and his wife prisoners in their own
kitchen.

The light was inadequate for an immediate trial and dispatch
of the fellow, so Cameron decided to wait until morning. With
the coming of day, they found the man to be in his early sixties,
silver-haired and rather gentle. The story which unfolded was
of a long struggle to protect the remnants of the cattle. There

had been repeated raids from the east, from the direction of Fort William. When asked why he had remained alone in this remote spot, the farmer replied, in a slow voice from the north of England, because of the fodder. Without the fodder the cattle would die. In any case the cattle could hardly be taken across the Bealach, and wouldn't it be suicidal to take them along the Quoich valley to the east? Cameron found about ten of the beasts in a tolerable condition, enough to be worth protecting. He decided to extend the range of MacKenzie's patrols so as to cover Glen Quoich, to supply the farm across the Bealach, and to give the farmer himself a choice. He explained that the cattle were now impounded. Either the man and his wife could cross unmolested into Kintail, leaving someone else to come over and tend the cattle, or he could stay on there, but working under rules of communal ownership. Unhesitatingly, the silver-haired farmer decided to stay. Saving the cattle, re-establishing the herd again, was his life—what else was there to live for?

Sometimes incidents which should have been simple turned out badly. With the coming of spring, and with the melting of the sea, inshore fishing became possible again. The catches were good, the problem being distribution—to minimize the time and effort needed to spread the catches evenly and fairly, to make sure that particular communities and crofts were not overlooked. It was in problems like this that Hamilton's "Doomsday Book" was proving its value.

To make the system work at all it was essential for the fishermen to hand over their catch immediately and without question. Three brothers in the Plockton region began to be difficult. Instead of handing over fish, they began distributing it themselves, operating their own barter system. Cameron impounded their boat, intending to hold it until the three should come to heel. Two days after a scene in which the boat was seized by main force, Cameron narrowly escaped being shot as he was

cycling the road into Kyle. The bullet hit the machine, over-
turned it and spilled him into the ditch, where he was reasonably protected from several further shots. Without proof there
was no action that Cameron cared to take himself. Others in
the community felt differently. One of the brothers was found
on the shore below a little cliff west of Plockton, his neck
broken. The other two escaped eastward through Achnasheen.

Cameron's relationship with Madeleine did not improve. The
root of the matter, Cameron knew, was that this whole way
of life did not suit his wife. It was too crude, too rough-hewn,
wholly unlike their past life in Geneva, at any rate in its outward forms.

The situation was not improved by the arrival of Janet and
by the circumstance that she was six months pregnant. She had
crossed from Strathfarrar through the glen north of Maoile
Lunndaidh, past Glennaig Lodge into Achnashellach, and then
to Lochcarron. The journey must have been hard and difficult
and only a desperate girl would have made it. Janet said her
parents were dead now, that everything to the east was in a
state of anarchy, that Cameron's activities were becoming known
everywhere, that she had somehow connected him with the
man in the car, and so had made the journey across the mountains. There was nothing else to be done, she said. Admiring the
girl for her determination, Cameron saw no reason to hide the
situation from Madeleine. He told her the facts plainly and un-
equivocally.

The break with Madeleine came unexpectedly, however, not
because of Janet but from a sheep-stealing incident. The cul-
prit, a sandy-haired man from the shores of Loch Long, claimed
his family was hungry, which was very likely true. Yet Cameron
had the thief hanged from one of the trees which grew along
the lochside. He waited himself by the tree as long as there was
any sign of life remaining in the wretched man, and then
made his way back to Ardelve.

He and Madeleine had one of the houses now. It was reasonably comfortable without being ostentatious. She was waiting for him as he came in stony-faced. He noticed a prayer book on the table in the little parlor where she confronted him. From the horror on her face he knew she must have heard of the hanging. "What has become of you?" she wailed.

"If I'd spared the man . . ." he began.

"*You* spare the man. Who are you to say that? Only God can give life and only God can take away life."

"Stupid words, woman. Haven't you read of age-old wars in which men gave themselves legalized sanction to take away life?"

"You hanged the man. *You.*" Madeleine's voice was stronger now.

"I was after telling you, if the man had gone free others would have taken the sheep. There are few enough now. Soon they would all have been taken."

"No sheep in the world is worth a human life." Madeleine was scornful now.

"This is the way of it," said Cameron in his grimmest tone. "A sheep is not worth a human life so long as there are many sheep. But the *last* sheep, the last sheep in the world, is worth *many* human lives."

He saw his words were having no effect and he regretted having broken his self-imposed rule never to explain.

"*Against the word of God it is,*" cried Madeleine in a fervent voice.

Cameron picked up the prayer book, "Aye, there is no shortage of men who are privy to the word of God. So they say themselves. But I have never heard anything from this God myself, only from the men who say they are privy to his word." He slapped the book violently down on the table.

"You should be on your knees. You should be on your knees, craving forgiveness from God," Madeleine panted, aghast at Cameron's sacrilegious treatment of the prayer book.

"I can hear anything this God has to say standing upright on my two feet, just as well as crawling on my knees."

Madeleine rushed at him, her eyes blazing, her arms outstretched. He hit her a hard slap across the cheek and said: "Shut yer blather, woman."

Sobbing uncontrollably, Madeleine rushed upstairs. Cameron had a strong urge to follow her to the bedroom and to take her forcibly. But he suspected the great strength of his sexual response was due to the hanging. Reflecting savagely that he didn't know how the God of Abraham would have behaved, he quit the house. He made his way to one of the boats and spent the night fishing on the loch.

Returning from Kyle the following day, Cameron found that Madeleine had gone. He made no attempt to follow her, or to have her followed, thinking she'd be back again within two or three days at most. A spell of physical misery, of being forced to come to terms willy-nilly with the new realities of life, would do her the world of good, he decided. But Madeleine did not return within two or three days. Inquiries, at first casual and then anxious, showed her to have made quick progress from Ardelve to Shiel. From there she had set out for Cluanie, evidently intent on breaking into the outside world. Cameron sent Toddy MacKenzie and two of his men in search of her, again thinking she would be found within a day or two. But Madeleine did not return. Neither did MacKenzie or his men.

It was this loss of his wife which first turned Cameron's attention seriously to the outside world. One part of him would have liked to follow her. Much as he felt her inadequate to the immediate present, she represented a way of life which Cameron desperately wished to recover. He stood for many hours gazing disconsolately from Cluanie toward the east. He decided he would move to the east, but not precipitately, for that was impossible—the loss of MacKenzie had shown the way it was. But he would make someone out there pay dearly for this loss of his wife. Cameron valued very few of his possessions. For these few he would wreak vengeance if they should be taken from him. Back in Ardelve he moved Janet into the house.

It was somewhere in the first half of June. There was uncertainty about the date to about a week, because nobody had yet reset the calendar to within a day's accuracy. Over the past six months odd scraps of news had gradually seeped in from outside. There had been news of disasters underground, within mines, caused by uncontrollable floods. Important people had been drowned and governments swept away, it was said. Cameron guessed this must be the result of attempts to seek refuge from radiation damage. There were still no organized radio broadcasts, indicating a state of total collapse to the south, collapse following disaster, with no recovery apparently.

Cameron had formed a clear picture of what must be happening now. Animals, at any rate the higher animals, could only have survived in a narrow belt stretching a few degrees north and south of the arctic circle. Odd pockets of survival would be distributed here and there along this belt: the north of Scotland, Norway, Sweden, parts of Russia, Canada, Iceland. Little else. Bacteria and plant life would be dominating the rest of the earth. The ground to the south would now be severely radioactive. Cameron had been much concerned with radioactive danger from the atmosphere, from tropical air blown north. Fortunately most of the particle radiation must have been "soft" and would not produce much in the way of long-lived nuclear species. There would be a good deal of carbon–14 in the air, coming from neutron capture by nitrogen, and this would appear in due course in their meager agricultural crops. Cameron had placed great emphasis on fish because he reckoned fish would be least affected.

The temptation everywhere among the isolated pockets of humanity would be to live on existing stores of food, fuel and clothing. Where the stores were largest the temptation would be strongest. It could seem as if stocks might last forever, but no stock or store would in fact last forever. Sooner or later people would be thrown onto their own resources, and the sooner the better. Cameron had seen this plainly from the beginning. He had seen that parasites, human parasites, would arise wherever stocks and stores were ample.

This was exactly what happened in the Inverness region. The resources of Inverness were much greater than those of the western valleys. They were sufficient to maintain all survivors through the winter and early spring. Stocks of petrol were the first to run short. Restricted groups were soon in control of the remaining petrol. The groups fought and preyed on each other until one emerged stronger and more dominant than the others. It was effectively organized on military lines by a man named Macready. Alistair Macready had been a captain in the British Army. He'd had experience ranging from riot control in the Middle East to the civil war in Northern Ireland, experience which he found well suited to the present situation. As Macready's gang became dominant the others withered away, their members now anxious to throw in their lot with Macready

Macready had started by raiding old Army, Air Force and Navy installations for weapons and vehicles. The automatic weapons, the four-wheel-drive vehicles equipped with radio communication, were sufficient for him to emerge in undisputed physical control of the wide range of territory centered on Inverness. His pseudo-military dominance interfered with any development of the kind which Cameron had achieved in the western valleys. Individuals with ideas of progressive reconstruction were prevented from cooperating together. With supplies of strategic materials growing scarcer, Macready became ever more concerned with directly punitive action. Farms and houses and people were destroyed whenever they became even a minor nuisance. Macready's initially rather hit-and-miss organization became more efficient, more autocratic and steadily more repressive. This was inevitable, because it was not imbued with any idea, except to live as a giant parasite on the countryside.

This was the organization with which Cameron knew he had

to deal. He had no taste for confronting Macready's automatic weapons with only his collection of old stalkers' rifles. Besides, with the scent of Culloden in his nostrils, he had no taste for fighting anywhere in the environs of Inverness. It thereafter followed that Macready must be made to come to him. The man must be provoked into a punitive action against the western valleys. The easiest route from Inverness would be along the remains of the Loch Luichart road to Achnasheen, then south down Glen Carron. Cameron pondered the problem of defending the Loch Luichart road.

He came to the somewhat paradoxical conclusion that it would be best to leave the easiest road open, but to close the harder ways, particularly Glen Moriston and Glen Garry. The advantage of leaving the easiest way open was that Macready would then be certain to take it. To know which way the man was coming would provide just the advantage he was seeking.

Cameron knew that for his first strike he could do pretty well anything he liked, so long as it was kept hidden until the final moment. So he resolved to hit Macready at his most sensitive spot. He sent thirty men into Inverness. They arrived at different times in ones and twos and they walked the roads only for the last mile or two, journeying essentially the whole way across the hills. They carried only small arms which remained concealed until they arrived simultaneously by the harbor, in front of Macready's main petrol dump. Within minutes they had dealt with the guard and exploded the dump. As they hoped might be the case, the guard had been possessed of a vehicle. They loaded captured automatic weapons into it. Four of them jumped aboard and drove off. The rest scattered immediately to the south, to walk the long way home along the east side of Loch Ness and up from Invergarry to Cluanie, which Cameron had equipped long ago as a strong point.

The men in the vehicle were prepared for a challenge. They took the road on the west side of Loch Ness, rather than the road to Achnasheen, because then they could easily stop and take to woods and hills which would lead them eventually back to Kintail. Since the raid was unexpected there was in fact no challenge. So they drove to Drumnadrochit and Cannich and as far toward Loch Affric as they could. The road had been bad all the way but it disintegrated entirely on the twists and turns below Loch Affric. They took out the guns and the vehicle's radio equipment and proceeded to topple the machine over a gorge into the river below. Then finally they had a heavy and long carry up the glen as far as Altbeath, which was also established now as a strong point.

For Macready the prospect of attacking the western valleys came as a relief. He was a man not much above middle height and rather thin, who always wore battle dress with red shoulder flashes. Macready had considerable intelligence, of a certain type, enough for him to see that, like a clockspring, his empire was gradually running down. He could have kept it going for quite a long time, and gone on having it good, if it hadn't been for the rats. Macready's intelligence was not of the kind to have foreseen that an army of hungry rats from all north Scotland would converge on his precious food reserves. Nor did he understand enough of the habits and the fierce determination of the rat to tackle the problem in an effective way. What he thought he saw now was how easy it would be, with his weapons and equipment, to take over the western valleys. Then he could go on having it good over there, the same as he'd had it good in Inverness. Cameron's attack triggered his intention.

After crossing many miles of boulder-strewn landscape, what was left of the road wound its way to the side of Loch Luichart, where it passed through a ribbonlike belt of trees some five miles long. The heavy dew of a July morning suffused the woodland. The sun was not yet high enough for direct rays to reach the road, when, with a roaring cacophony, Macready's column of motor vehicles crawled to the entrance of the tree belt. Perhaps a dozen men of the four hundred in the column jumped to the ground. Some were in rough clothes of no particular description, others were in tattered battle dress like their leader. The men didn't like the thick trees with the dark loch to the left and the steep rocky hillside rearing up high to the right.

Macready, dark and scowling, a remnant of a cigarette in the corner of his mouth, decided he had nothing worse than a nuisance here. It never crossed his mind to turn back. In any case he'd decided he wasn't going back, although his men didn't know this yet. With a contemptuous jerk of the thumb he indicated the column should proceed. The men on the ground swung themselves back into the carriers, the engines roared loud again, and the column heaved its way over a small rocky outcrop which marked the entrance to the wood.

Inside the wood a dim light and air heavy with moisture made sharp contrast with the world outside. At each corner of the twisting track the driver of the leading carrier peered anxiously ahead. On and on the vehicles rolled at no more than a walking pace. Still there was no obstruction—one mile, two miles. To Macready's men, standing packed tight, it seemed they must soon be through and in clear country again. But the drivers knew from frequent glances at their instruments that this was not so, that in fact they were little beyond the mid-point of the passage.

At last a big fir lay felled across the narrow pothole-strewn road. With winches and ample manpower they could shift it, but the operation would take time. Within minutes Macready had his forces deployed. A hundred men with automatic rifles broke out of the woodland to the right. Here they had a clear view up the hillside. Protected by this guard, the rest of the men busied themselves with shifting the tree.

A shot, strangely deadened by the heavy air, came from the trees ahead. A man, engaged a moment ago in fastening a rope, sprawled on the ground. Within seconds the men around the vehicle sprayed the area with bursts of fire. As if in response, a tall gaunt man broke into the open, jumping down to the road, but at a point only a yard or two from where the road turned to the right and passed immediately out of sight. In a flash the big thin fellow was away around this corner. Macready's men blazed at their now invisible target. Then in response to a fiercely shouted command they started in pursuit.

The gaunt man had quit the trees for the road to make it possible for him to outflank the men guarding the open hillside—they stumbled among boulders while he simply ran freely along the track. Five hundred yards along, still clutching his long-barreled rifle, the fellow plunged back into the wood, at a spot where an open ride made for easy access to the hillside. Although he was now several hundred yards ahead of Macready's guard, shots rippled over the ground and he was glad to reach a steep-sided ghyll, the bottom of which gave excellent cover. The ghyll was really a gash in the hillside, steepening and becoming more deeply indented toward the top.

Macready's men soon reached the eastern shoulder of the ghyll. It was immediately clear that to climb the open hillside would be much quicker than to plunge down to the rough stream bed at the bottom of the ghyll. All they needed to do was to climb the open hillside until they were above the thin man. Some of them crossed to the western side of the ghyll and also began to climb upward. They had their quarry hemmed in this way.

The gaunt man in the stream bed had discarded his rifle now. His long legs were making remarkably fast pace over the difficult ground. From time to time his pursuers had momentary glimpses of his progress. At first they wasted time shooting at an impossible target. Then they gave themselves to climbing the hill as fast as possible. Inevitably they began to string out, the faster ones going ahead more and more as the gradient steepened. The natural instinct of the hunter forced them to maximum effort. The strongest and fittest led the way, gradually opening a space between themselves and the others.

A friend of the gaunt man, also a former stalker by profession, lay hidden in the rocks, waiting. The moment had arrived now. Raising his rifle, he sighted it and squeezed the trigger in one slow continuous movement. The leading member of the pursuing party jerked backward, his automatic weapon clattering on the rocks.

The first thoughts of Macready's men were to throw themselves to the ground, and then to start shooting. But at what? Gradually it dawned on them that this hillside could shelter scores of expert marksmen, which is exactly what it did. Scarcely half of the pursuit party managed to return to the wood below, by which time the advantage had been shifted.

With strenuous curses the men piled into the vehicles again, except that from now on a score of them walked ahead of the crawling, roaring column with the intention of flushing out any lurking sniper. They made several hundred yards before reaching the second obstacle, another tree across the road. At last it occurred to Macready to send a strong party forward for the whole length of the ribbonlike wood. They reported nineteen similar blockages.

Macready began to calculate time. Reckoning one hour for shifting each tree—the first one had taken twice as long as that but they'd shorten the time with practice—he calculated a delay of a day, no more. All he need do was to make sure no more trees were felled across the road. Macready ordered patrols to cover the whole of the remaining two miles from their present position to the western end of the wood. The disposition of the remaining three hundred and fifty men was now a hundred outside the wood on the lower part of the hillside, another hundred, two for every fifty yards, on the road ahead of the vehicles, fifty guarding the rear, and the remaining hundred to shift the trees one by one. The system worked to Macready's satisfaction until it became dark in the wood. By this time more than half of the fallen trees had been removed.

But as the light faded, the guards ahead of the vehicles, two to every fifty yards, became sitting ducks for those of Cameron's men who had lain all day waiting in the dense undergrowth. Hidden in the dark with captured automatic rifles, they still bided their time. They waited almost two hours while a campfire was lit and while their enemies ate and relaxed. Then they raked the camp and the road ahead of the vehicles with their own deadly fire.

Macready gave no command. Nor was there any reason for him to do so, since it was obvious to his men that safety lay only in scattering themselves into the dark surrounding woodland. The assailants from the west took the opportunity of the confusion to shower petrol bombs among the stationary vehicles. Then they worked their way stealthily out onto the hillside. In the gloom of a July night they moved slowly up the hill to join the rest of Cameron's advanced force. In all, there were no more than a hundred of them.

With the coming of daylight the balance of fire power swung decisively back to Macready's party. Although many of their enemies were dead, Cameron's men on the hill still dared not attempt a direct attack. Nor did they need do so, for during the night the road had been decisively blocked by a further mass of fallen trees, not only to the west of the vehicles but to the east now as well.

Macready had reached a state of indecision. The endless trees were confusing him. Through another day the pattern repeated and at night the wood was again infiltrated. For the second night his men had to lie low, without having a target to aim at, but themselves targets. It was not until the third morning, with two-thirds of his vehicles burned out or inoperative, that Macready at last understood why he was so much at a disadvantage. He saw what he should have seen from the beginning—that his vehicles were trapped but his men were not. They could all simply walk out of the wood. He'd been desperately loath to reach this conclusion because his mobility would be gone—the mobility which had given him so much power. He gave orders to continue westward on foot, moving the whole of his force outside the wood on to the lower part of the hillside.

From high on the hill, Cameron counted the number of his adversary. Roughly two hundred and thirty. Almost down to half. Cameron understood perfectly the military tactics of dividing the enemy—divide and destroy, piece by piece. As he watched the men below, stumbling through boulders, weighted by heavy weapons, he thought grimly of the road ahead of them. He thought of the hostile rocky pass awaiting them if they should continue westward from Achnasheen. He thought of the long thin shore of Loch Maree. He thought of the even thicker forest below Achnashellach if they should decide to go south. He shook his head. Macready had been no problem. The rats would give him more trouble.

12

The Ruined Cathedral

The logistic problems of the Inverness region were similar to the ones Cameron had already dealt with in the western valleys. They were bigger, but against this he was backed now by many months of experience, and by several scores of men whom he could trust, in both ability and character.

The psychological problems were bigger now, partly because the surviving population was larger, but also because everything had got off to a bad start. There was a serious lack of communal discipline. This showed up straightaway. There was nothing to be done with the rats except to poison them. The only way to do this was to put poison in the food stores which they were ravaging. Since there was no possibility of using anything except a crude poison—there happened to be a good stock of oxalic acid to hand, which would attack humans as well as rats—this meant the food would then be lost. Cameron, with his ruthless logic, saw the food was lost anyway. He ordered it poisoned. But there were many hungry people who now hated him for doing so.

Cameron had often thought about Duncan Fraser. Duncan had always accepted Cameron's instructions but had never come voluntarily to him, not since the burning of the corpses at Letterfearn. It was the same childlike irrationality.

There were three surviving clan chieftains in the region. It was clear they didn't like Cameron's way of running things but they accepted his leadership, partly because of his heredity and partly because they had no choice. He knew them by sight and that was all, for he had never in the past shown any liking for Anglicized clan gatherings.

The passing months were marked by a few special events. Janet gave birth to a boy. Cameron, hitherto childless, was tempted to play—perhaps to overplay—the proud father. There was always a lurking doubt in his mind, about whether he really was the father. But he saw no logical reason why not. Anyway, what did it matter so long as the boy was healthy?

The saddest time came from something which didn't happen. Cameron made a strenuous effort to find the girl who had placed the flower on the Culloden grave, but he could find no trace of her or of her mother. He finally gave up the quest, convinced they must have perished in the storms, or the heat, or the cold, or from the hands of marauders. He had the plantation of scrubby trees on the Culloden battlefield put to the fire. He walked to the Moor, for the fourth time now, and watched as the trees burned. There was a wind blowing which drove the flames. Listening to the fierce ripping of the fire, Cameron thought it had taken a long time, more than two hundred years, for the position to be righted—there was no line of Hanoverian regiments to worry him now. He stood by the old graves facing the flames. For a long blurred moment it seemed as if the girl came riding past on her bicycle once more. Perhaps it was she who had been the ghost.

There are about five miles where the Ness River flows from the northern end of the loch to the town of Inverness itself. The river flows through a grassy parkland. Cameron was walking the parkland one autumn day when the matter of immediate concern suddenly jumped from his mind as he caught sight of a figure in the distance. His keen sight already picked out a cap slanted forward on the head. Breaking into a run, he shouted, "Toddy! Toddy MacKenzie!"

The two men greeted each other. To Cameron it seemed as though MacKenzie had stepped out of yesterday. Except for a leaner, rangier look there was no change. The same cap, the same cigarette.

"Ye'll be after wondering about the wife?"

"Aye."

"Well, she's fine, Mr. Cameron."

"Where is she?"

"To the south."

"But where?"

Toddy scratched his head, pulling the cap forward. "Mr. Cameron, ye'll not be understanding what I'm telling ye now. But its unco' strange to the south."

"How far south?"

"Pitlochry. There isn't much further than that."

"You've seen it all?"

"Aye."

MacKenzie stood there rolling another cigarette. Cameron remembered how in the very first days Toddy had been away over to Glenelg. Toddy the nomad would never have been satisfied until he'd seen it all.

"How is it, at the end?"

"Water, floods and flies."

"South of Pitlochry."

"Aye."

"And my wife's all right?"

"Aye, she's fine."

"Why didn't you bring her back?"

"Well, it was like this, Mr. Cameron." Toddy stood there lighting his cigarette. Cameron waited, thinking that getting information from Toddy was as bad as pulling teeth.

"By the time I came with your lady, Mr. Cameron, there were men behind me, men wi' guns, ye'll understand."

"A fellow called Macready?"

"That'll be the name."

"Man, ye missed a bonnie fight."

"I'm regretting it, Mr. Cameron."

"Couldn't you have brought her back—in spite of Mac-ready?"

"If she'd been willing, I could."

"So you went on with her?"

"Aye."

"Until she was safe?"

"Aye."

"And after that you had a look around yourself?"

"Aye, that was the way of it, Mr. Cameron."

"Toddy, I want you to bring her back home now. You can have plenty of men."

"I could, Mr. Cameron. But I'm thinking it would be better if you were to come yourself."

"Why?"

"Like I said, it's unco' strange. The lads I took wi' me are dead, Mr. Cameron. But they didn't die in a fair fight."

Cameron found he could press MacKenzie no further. Toddy was willing to guide a party south, but he was reluctant to be its leader, for a reason he wouldn't explain and which Cameron couldn't understand.

There was no prospect for many a long month of Cameron going south himself. He had a hard and difficult winter to see through. So for a while he dismissed the thought from his mind. Madeleine was alive and apparently well according to MacKenzie. In any case she had gone south of her own free will.

It wasn't until seeds had been planted the following spring that he was able to return to the problem of Madeleine. To make a journey to Pitlochry and back should, he calculated, take about a month. Not for straight walking alone, but for all the delays and detours and possibly for arguments with Madeleine herself. It was a month he could ill spare, but

166

Madeleine was his wife. She might be "fine," whatever being "fine" was, but he had to make sure. He had to see her before he would know whether he should simply leave her or bring her back by main force.

The first problem was to decide how many men to take. The smaller the party, the greater its mobility. There would be difficulty with food if he were to march an army corps. Yet Toddy MacKenzie's curious warnings suggested that the party be not too small. Cameron decided on thirty men, himself and Toddy excepted. They were all veterans of the Loch Luichart battle. Among them was the gaunt thin man, old Angus Mac-Lennan.

They carried a fair amount of food. To keep the weight down Cameron went as light on weapons as he dared. Two long-range rifles, small arms for every man, and three boxes of grenades from Macready's armament. They took two of the only five mules in the whole Inverness region. They walked the ruined A9 road through Carrbridge and Aviemore to Kincraig. Here they went directly south, up the Feshie valley, then east to White Bridge, and thence into upper Glentilt.

As they moved down the Tilt they found people, not many, occupying the ruined buildings of what had once been prosperous farms. After many miles over barren rocks and moor, with the Cairngorms under a heavy cover of ice and snow, they were glad to make contact with humans again, although they found even the women taciturn. There was a curious look about them, which Cameron connected with the strangeness Toddy had warned him about. He had a feeling of them not looking "right," whatever that might mean.

The party made its way without undue haste into the lower Tilt. After descending a steep piece of woodland approaching Blair Atholl, they came suddenly into open ground. Immediately ahead was a large group of armed men. Cameron was instantly angry with himself for not sending Angus and two or three of his party scouting ahead. He'd simply followed Toddy Mac-Kenzie more or less blindly because he felt Toddy knew more about this country than he did. Not that the weapons carried by these men need worry him very much. They had a few guns but mostly they were carrying swords. Some had only rough pikes fashioned from farm implements. It would have been easy to cope with them at long range. The trouble, Cameron saw immediately, was that they were too close now. His own men, equipped with the grenades, could blast a way through, but being outnumbered ten to one, there would be serious casualties at this short range. Cameron decided to wait a while before making a move.

The ranks ahead parted and a man on a chestnut horse came forward. The sight unnerved Cameron, for he had long been sure he'd never see a horse again.

"Where are ye from?" asked the man.

"The north."

"And where are ye going?"

"South. We seek nothing from ye. I'll be glad if ye'd ask yer men to stand aside."

"So ye come in peace?"

"Aye, we come in peace."

"Then I'll not let it be said ye passed through my land without being given food and shelter."

"We have a long way to go."

"Aye, and ye'll travel the faster for some warm food. I am the Lord Moray."

Cameron bowed. "My name is Cameron."

The man on horseback lifted an arm by way of salute. Then he instructed his men to break into two groups. One group marched to the right, the other to the left of Cameron's men as they followed behind the horseman. This might have been the opportunity for a showdown, but Cameron was loathe to break the ancient rules of Highland hospitality which his host seemed so determined to honor. Half an hour later they arrived at a castle. There was an extensive grass lawn in surprisingly good condition at the front, where a wide flight of stone steps led into the building itself. Parts were collapsed but most of it seemed to be occupied. This would be Blair Castle.

Dismounting by the stone steps, Moray handed the bridle to a servant. Turning to Cameron, he said, "Ye, Cameron, and yer man will be following me. The others will be shown their quarters."

This was according to the rules. Cameron was permitted an attendant who could remain armed, to make sure that he, Cameron, wasn't stabbed from behind—while drinking. The rest of his men would be fed in the big kitchen. They would be expected to sit down to the evening meal unarmed—since they came ostensibly in peace—although they could maintain a watch on their arms if they chose to do so.

Cameron selected Ian Bàn, a strong, good-looking lad in his early twenties. He thought for a moment of Toddy but changed his mind when he noticed a flash in MacKenzie's eye. He addressed Angus in Gaelic.

"*Put a guard on the weapons and see the men do not drink.*" Then, dropping his voice, he added, "*Find a reason to come to the dining hall.*"

"What was that?" Moray asked as they walked up the stone staircase.

"I was giving orders to guard the weapons."

"Those are not the words of a friend, Cameron."

"It is a discipline I cannot relax, even for you, my lord."

A servant showed Cameron and Ian Bàn up a long flight of stairs and along a corridor to a large room at the rear of the castle. Within minutes other servants had brought half a dozen jugs of hot water. From the speed of their delivery, Cameron had the impression the fellows must literally be running about their business.

169

After their long march they were glad to wash themselves down. Cameron was staring at himself in the mirror, thinking the beard he'd grown over the past months had given him a thoroughly villainous look, when a cry came from the courtyard outside. Cameron wrenched a window open just as the cry was repeated.

"What was that?" asked Ian Bàn, his face white.

"It came from those stables over there. It sounded like a woman."

Cameron waited by the window. Some minutes later a man came from the stables. He watched carefully as the fellow crossed the courtyard below.

"Should we do something?"

"Not for the moment, Ian lad. We'll see what we can do later."

A wood fire was burning in a great fireplace when Cameron and Ian came downstairs. Moray was waiting.

"Ye'll be feeling better now," he said.

"Much better, thank you, my lord."

Moray poured two whiskies. One he handed to Cameron, the other he kept for himself, ignoring Ian Bàn.

The room was paneled, with the polished woodwork shining brightly in the firelight.

"Slainté!" boomed Cameron, snapping the whisky and thinking it a long day since he'd taken a drop as mellow as this.

"Slainté!" responded Moray, also lowering the whisky, but more in a steady drink than a snap.

"I'll be asking ye, would ye be *the* Cameron now?"

"I would."

"Traveling with but a score of men—eh?"

Cameron noticed the edge of scorn in his host's voice. "He who travels light travels fast, my lord."

"Aye, so long as he travels at all."

Moray poured more whisky. Cameron lifted his glass against

the fire. "If I wasn't in an awful hurry I'd be glad to bide awhile here," he said.

"Ye would."

"Aye, ye've got a fine place here, my lord."

"Ye've got nothing like this?"

"I haven't. Only a few stone cottages. It's poor country away to the north."

"Aye, and not many men, I'm thinking."

Cameron snapped the whisky again. Unless Moray happened to have a remarkable head, he felt he would be gaining an advantage with every glass they consumed. But Moray didn't drink this time. He moved toward a door, saying, "May I present the Lady Moray?"

Through a wide-opened door there came a girl of nineteen or twenty. She wore a long rustling gown bare at the shoulders. She had the overwhelming loveliness which Cameron had seen only once or twice before in his lifetime. He stepped forward, bowed and kissed the outstretched hand. "I'm honored, your ladyship," he said, thinking Moray must be as old as he was.

"I'm glad you came," she replied in a level voice.

Two servants immediately opened another door.

"Shall we go in, Cameron?"

Moray led the way into the dining hall, while Cameron offered his arm to the girl. There was a long polished oak table set at one end with three big chairs. Cameron escorted the girl to the right side, moving the heavy chair for her. Then he went round to the left, leaving the head position for Moray. Ian Bàn came behind Cameron, and so was placed immediately opposite the girl. The lad, Cameron could see, had been unnerved and shattered by the girl. Ian now would be unlikely to react quickly in an emergency. The table was plentifully laid with silverware. The candlelit scene, with firelight flickering in the distance, suggested a charming and relaxed evening, a kind of return to a former, better-favored world.

Cameron knew it would be otherwise. He knew it from the three men standing behind Moray, close by a plastered wall which reflected the flames of the candles. The one immediately behind Moray was the man Cameron had seen coming from the stables.

"Now I'll be asking ye, Cameron, how would ye be seeing the future of Scotland?"

"I'd be seeing it as a return to the old days."

"Aye, and so we'll be needing . . ."

"We'll be needing a leader, won't we, Moray?"

"Ye hear what he says," Moray said to the girl.

"I've been thinking, the Lady Moray here would make a bonny queen, wouldn't she now?"

Cameron caught the girl's eyes. The fear stared at him now. With the coming of darkness a formless but all-pervasive fear had suffused the castle. Cameron could see it in the servants who were scurrying back and forth with food and plates. He could feel it in the hard oak table and he could see it in the candlelight. He fancied he could hear it in a thin wind which soughed outside the castle walls. He was beginning to understand now what Toddy MacKenzie had meant when he'd said the south was "unco' strange." He knew now why Toddy had led him straight here down the Tilt. He knew why the servants bringing his hot water *had* been running.

"And what might ye be thinking now, Cameron?"

"About how we could divide up Scotland, you and me."

"Were ye now?"

"Aye, and I was thinking I'd like a place like this. Maybe your lady here has a sister. . . ."

Moray broke into a laugh, ending in the high pitch of a madman. Cameron saw at last how every survivor from the days of the inferno had been faced by a watershed, one way leading to insanity, the other back to sanity. He himself had instinctively taken the sane route when he'd burned the corpses at Letterfearn. His dominance of the men of the Shiel valley had forced them into a total sanity which had then taken all the western valleys the same way. Macready had gone the other way; Macready had been insane right up to the moment when they'd pitched him into the steep gorge above Achnashellach. But Macready's brand of insanity had been a mild affair compared to this appalling thing here.

"So ye're wanting a woman, are ye?" inquired Moray.

"I'm hot for one, and that's the truth."

Moray turned in his chair, giving the merest nod to the sinister figure behind him. The fellow gave a sleazy grin, and moved to quit the room. Cameron called him back. "I like mine nicely dressed," he roared, half pointing across the table at the girl. Finding fancy clothes for the unfortunate woman they intended to produce would keep the sadistic bastard away for an extra half hour.

"And are there no women in the north?"

"Not as many. Not much choice and not so pretty."

Cameron again pointed his whisky glass across the table. By admitting to a lust he didn't feel, he'd achieved three things. He'd put Moray off his guard, he'd got rid of one of his attendants, and he'd surely brought Ian Bàn back to his senses.

In the south here things had gone the other way, thought Cameron. Perhaps slowly at first, then with increasing momentum, the south had pitched into communal insanity. It was "unco' strange" all right. Moray was a phony, usurping a great name, a sadistic madman who had fastened himself like an iron vise on a distraught community. Mad in direction, but overwhelmingly cunning in tactics. Cameron's party would have been mauled in a fight outside in the field but they would have come out best in the end. This self-styled Moray had managed with his usurped name to change a basically lost position into one which now carried acute danger for Cameron and his men.

"Ye hear the wind outside, Moray?"

It pained Cameron to continue using the name but caution demanded he should hold himself in check yet awhile.

"I hear it."

"Ye know what that is?"

"What else but the wind?"

"I'll tell ye what it is, Moray. Ye're listening now to the cry of damned souls." He heard a swift intake of breath from the girl. "Aye, damned souls, Moray. The souls of the folk who died in the great heat."

"Ye're havers, man."

"Haven't ye realized we're all dead now, Moray?"

In the early days Cameron had asked himself this question quite seriously. He gave it out now in a hollow voice well suited to the evil atmosphere of the place. There came a choking sob from the girl.

"I'm asking ye to explain that, Cameron."

"This is the life beyond, Moray."

"I'm finding it a grand life."

"Maybe ye deserved it then."

"That's what I'm thinking."

"And maybe I was deserving what happened to me."

"Aye, man."

"I have the hand of death on me, Moray. It lies dark across my eyes."

"I tell ye, ye're havers, man."

Cameron reached out and gripped Moray's arm. One of the men against the wall moved a pace forward but Ian Bàn blocked his path. Then the third of Moray's attendants was back, forcing a girl ahead of him. Cameron cursed his stupidity for not making better use of the past few minutes. He'd managed to disturb Moray, but not enough.

Cameron got up from his chair—at least he'd a good reason to move about the room now. He went immediately to the new girl and lifted her head. It was another beautiful face, but crushed and tragic.

"She'll have been well used," he stated brutally.

There was laughter behind the table.

"Isn't she good enough for you, Cameron?"

"As good as she was for you, Moray."

Cameron rose to his full height in red anger now, all caution gone. "Aye, one lass finished and another just beginning," he continued.

"Ye'll be regretting that." Moray had risen and the men behind the table moved forward. Cameron fingered the pin of the grenade in his pocket.

"I said death was across my eyes, Moray. I meant just that." Cameron's baleful tone carried total conviction. The men checked themselves, and as they did so there came a long moan from outside.

The main door of the dining hall, a heavy solid timber, burst open. The tall, infinitely thin gray figure of Angus MacLennan stood silhouetted there. He seemed to be fighting for breath. He clawed his way to the center of the room, followed silently by three more of Moray's men and by Toddy MacKenzie. MacLennan towered there, half a head above Cameron, his cheeks visible in the firelight but the deep eye sockets dark like a skull. He raised his hands to a seemingly impossible height and croaked, "It's here, Cameron. The ghost of the great one is here."

Cameron sprang to the table close beside Moray. "Did I no' tell ye. Death is here, man." In horror he pointed. "Look Moray, behind ye!"

The girl from the stable was the first to scream. Then the other girl began to shriek in long, blood-chilling spasms. There behind the table was a monstrous shape, forming and reforming, but always with a skull-like face. Unlike the skull face of Angus MacLennan, light now shone from the eye sockets.

Moray reared toward the thing. It hovered high in the air like an obscene vulture. Then strong hands clutched at Moray's throat. Cameron heard a gurgle, the upwelling of blood, and Moray crashed across the table.

Toddy MacKenzie leaped like a flame on the man who had brought in the second girl. Cameron's quick eyes saw the dirk go in. From the expresison on her face the girl must have seen it too. It was an expression which could have been mistaken for religious ecstasy.

"Get the girl out. She's yours now," Cameron whispered to Ian Bàn. He pushed the second girl toward MacKenzie.

"Get her out, Toddy."

With Angus beside him, Cameron backed slowly to the door of the hall, covering the retreat of the others. Nobody moved until they were gone. Then the five remaining men fell hungrily on the silverware.

Explosions now rent the castle. Cameron's men came outside, half a dozen at a time. Within an hour he had them together. His party had experienced physical bruising and they'd taken a thoroughly bad scare. With the two girls they moved quickly down into Blair Atholl. A mile or so farther south they found a rough shelter, where they settled down for the night. Wary now, Cameron set a guard and settled himself to sleep on the hard ground. His thoughts strayed to the soft beds he was sure must be up there in the castle. He could have a place like that for himself. Odd he'd never realized it.

He thought about Toddy MacKenzie, damning Toddy for his reticence. The man must have known all along just where he'd been leading the party. The trouble, Cameron now saw, lay in his own spectacular success. Toddy had never contemplated the possibility of failure. Cameron thought how very near he'd been to disaster that night. But not quite. He smiled at himself in the dark, recalling the many boyhood hours he'd spent with lamps and candles. He had been learning the principles of optics then. He'd practiced and practiced until he could throw almost any kind of image with his hands. The glowing skull on the wall had been child's play, literally. He'd seen the possibility from the moment of entering the dining hall, but he hadn't found a way to use it until Angus made his superb intervention. Cameron remembered the gaunt figure with a shiver and then fell asleep.

With the coming of daylight the party sorted itself out. They marched through Killiecrankie to Pitlochry, with scouts out now, but there was no sign of a sortie from Blair Atholl. It was likely the situation there would just run itself down like an unwinding clock spring. Other repressive groups would soon arise, inevitably, for without strong communal responsibility there could be no other kind of society. In spite of the difficulties of extending himself across the Cairngorms and across the wastes of Rannoch, Cameron saw he must take in the south, otherwise he would always have this source of mental derangement on his flank.

MacKenzie led them east from Pitlochry. Cameron had a presentiment now of where they were going. He thought about asking Toddy, but checked himself at the last moment and said instead, "I've been thinking, Toddy—that will have been the place where you had the trouble before."

"Aye, Mr. Cameron. I thought if ye were there . . ."

"I reckon we made it up now."

"We did, Mr. Cameron."

They trudged on, Toddy well pleased with himself.

From Straloch they took the winding road north. For a long time Cameron had plagued himself with the notion that Madeleine had joined some religious group. Until now the radio-telescope had never occurred to him. He saw at last why Toddy had found the situation difficult to explain.

They caught sight of the telescope from afar off, standing mute against the sky. As they drew nearer Cameron saw the supporting pillars had become badly twisted—this would be from the weight of ice which must have piled on it. At a glance he knew the instrument would never turn again.

Fielding's house was still there. Fielding himself came to meet them. He was tall like Cameron and he still wore heavy glasses. On the occasion of Cameron's earlier visit he had been an ample man. Now he was almost as thin as Angus MacLennan. His old suit hung on him like a cloth on a peg.

"Glad to see you back, Cameron," he said, as if nothing had happened. Then Madeleine ran from the house.

"Oh, my dear," she cried as she threw herself into Cameron's arms. He could feel that Madeleine had gone thin too. His men made a meal. He watched Madeleine and Fielding as they ate, very carefully.

Afterward, Fielding took him aside.

"I'd like to show you the telescope," he said. "It's badly damaged but it isn't irretrievable."

As in a dream, Cameron followed Fielding close by the telescope, just as he had done so long ago.

"I can make transit observations," explained Fielding.

"Of what?"

"That's just it. I need your help."

"My help?"

"Madeleine tells me that you have a lot of influence."

"Well?"

"Do you realize," exclaimed Fielding, staring up at the twisted structure, "that if we could change the elevation by only two degrees I'd be able to get the Crab Nebula?"

Mad, thought Cameron, totally mad.

"You'd need a lot of manpower."

"That's just it, Cameron. You can see I can't shift it myself."

"How do you manage for power—for the receivers?"

"Generators. I've still got a little diesel oil, but I have to ιse it very sparingly. That's another thing I'd like you to get for me—more diesel."

"How about food?"

"That's not so important, is it?"

"You have to live."

"The people around here—they're very kind. They give us food."

"From time to time?"

"Yes, from time to time."

Totally mad. But a better form of madness than the others', thought Cameron. Perhaps even an essential kind of madness.

Fielding looked him closely in the eye, the Ancient Mariner to the life. "I've something to show you, Cameron."

The voice was lowered, confidential and secretive, although there wasn't a soul to be seen within half a mile of where they were standing. Fielding put a hand on Cameron's arm and led him to the only bit of the old laboratory still standing. The interior was a disordered mass of electronics.

"Well, what is it?" Cameron asked.

"I've got tapes of the thing, Cameron, right to the *end*."

Fielding smiled, as if he'd just scored a scientific triumph.

"To the end?"

"Until the ice came."

"Through all the heat?"

"Yes. I had it on automatic tracking all the time."

"I see."

Cameron remembered the astronomer's abiding passion for observation and shook his head.

"I'd like to show you those tapes on a video scan, Cameron."

Fielding began to assemble various items of the electronics. He wasn't particularly skilled at it. Cameron became impatient.

"Let me do it. You tell me what you want," he said.

Cameron worked for several hours. This had once been his

life. In his time he'd built, or helped to build, several of the world's greatest physical machines. But it was gone now, the old life, except for an odd moment like this. He found himself assembling the electronic bits without effort, hardly listening to Fielding. At length he was satisfied with the lash-up, so he and Fielding started the generator. Fielding then ran sample bits of the tapes. When Fielding would have stopped Cameron kept him going.

"But there's really very little diesel left now. Surely you've seen enough," Fielding protested.

"I'll get you more diesel," Cameron insisted.

Eventually they switched everything off and returned grave-faced to the house.

Cameron jerked his thoughts back to Madeleine. She had sought out the one place, perhaps the one place in the whole world, where some connection with the old life could be found. She'd never expressed any particular interest in science and yet she had found the one place where science in the old sense was still thought important. For this she had been willing to live near starvation point. A paradox, still another form of madness. Cameron shook his head. She would have to come back now, by force if need be, if only because of the starvation. Cameron found himself wishing he could also shift the radiotelescope. The madness was even touching him now.

Rather to Cameron's surprise, Madeleine agreed to return. He noticed her packing away the prayer book, the one he'd given a good banging to almost a year ago now. She must have carried it the whole length of the hard road across Scotland.

The cavalcade set off along the track down to Straloch. Fielding asked to go with them a part of the way—to see what he could forage in the Kirkmichael valley, Cameron at first supposed. Reaching Straloch, Cameron thought to go east before turning north—the route through the Spittal of Glenshee, Braemar and Tomintoul would be less likely to involve incidents such as the one at Blair Atholl. But at Straloch, Madeleine insisted they go west. She refused to explain why, but kept on saying she would return north on condition they traveled first to Dunkeld. Fielding continued to accompany them.

There were other travelers on the road to Dunkeld, it seemed. People, ordinary folk, were walking the road in twos and threes. They always scattered immediately to the sides as soon as they saw the nature and number of Cameron's band. It took three days to reach Dunkeld. They came down into the town and found a crowd of shabbily dressed people already assembled there.

"I came for the Easter service," said Madeleine. "I didn't tell you, because you don't believe in it," she stated defiantly.

Dunkeld Cathedral was now largely open to the sky. Much of the external stonework had come down. The interior contained a few chairs but mostly the congregation had to stand. A few of the organ registers had been made to work again, enough to accompany the singing. The singing rose high to the broken rafters and out to the sky as it came in full from almost a thousand people. Cameron had embarrassed Madeleine by coming, and because Cameron had come so had most of his men. Two vergers had requested them to leave their arms outside but Cameron, after being once caught, would have none of it. He simply shouldered his way inside, to Madeleine's greater embarrassment. Fielding came too, since this was the real reason for his journey.

Cameron watched the people around him. He watched them sing. He watched Madeleine searching her prayer book. Fielding surprised him. In a way it had all started with Fielding. Cameron thought of the people who had followed him: Nygaard, Almond and the young astronomers—the astronomers so keen to observe, but not understanding that they were peering into the very mouth of hell. Mallinson and the government, preserving continuity until the last possible moment, finding themselves overwhelmed by a roaring flood in some remote mine or cave. Tom MacLean . . . MacLean's agonizing journey to Fort William had been for nothing—the injured man had not been able to survive the heat. Janet and her baby . . . The dead and the living.

Someone started to talk from an improvised pulpit. Cameron had no use for talk, only for the singing. He pushed his way into the main aisle and walked without haste from the cathedral. He walked across the bridge into Birnam and then up through woods toward the eastern ridge of the Tay valley. Although in the old days he'd driven the valley many times, he'd never walked above it before. In the old days the way up had looked quite long, but Cameron was so much harder now that it seemed little more than a stride before he was out on open hillside far above the river.

Macbeth's castle was supposed to have been on this eastern wall of the valley. Cameron found himself wondering where it might have been. He had gone perhaps a mile along the crest of the ridge when a familiar sound set his blood racing. For a year now Cameron had risen each day at dawn. Never once in this time had bird song greeted his ears. The creatures of the air seemed inexorably gone, extinct. But now a skylark soared above his head. He ran toward it. Then he remembered the skylark's trick of leading intruders away from its nest. He went back along the ridge, his keen eyes raking the ground. He searched the long grass as he had done hundreds of times in his boyhood. He found the nest, lined with hair, cunningly set below a small tussock. In it were three small eggs, speckled brown on white. Three eggs wholly without price. Cameron reached down and then drew quickly back, not daring to touch them. He pushed the green back around the nest and ran once more toward the bird, which soared again into the sky. It led him a long way and then disappeared at last. He sat on the grass for a while. When he came out of a reverie he found tears streaming down his face.

Cameron strode quickly back down the hillside. Immediately above Dunkeld he stopped. A bell was tolling from the cathedral. The tone was hollow and Cameron thought the bell had probably fallen and cracked. He sat listening and shaking his head. He had a heavier burden to bear than the poor souls down there. To them the whole course of the inferno had been strange and inexplicable, except in the crudest terms—God pouring down fire on Sodom and Gomorrah. Cameron had followed the thing step by step, detail by detail. It was all entirely rational and natural—up to a particular point. Cameron had never been able to understand the onset of total entire darkness. The temperature had fallen, not as night followed day, but with night following night. Degree by degree the temperature fell over almost a month until through the length and breadth of the land the mountains became buried in thick snowfields.

Cameron had never found a natural explanation for the termination of the great heat or for the descent of total darkness.

Now he knew the explanation to be rational but not natural. He knew an intelligence, a creature, had intervened at their direst moment. It was as if a man should hold up a hand to shield a moth as it flew near a candle. The moth could not understand how or why it came to be saved, as Cameron had failed to understand why the earth had been saved. Just as man was a creature of a different order to the moth, so a creature of a different order to man had intervened, intervened perhaps everywhere throughout the galaxy, intervened to protect the little creatures of the universe.

The hollow tones of the bell continued. If the people leaving the cathedral down there were to suspect what Cameron knew to be true they would instantly rush back inside. They would fall prostrate in ecstasy as they contemplated the power of their God. But Cameron knew this was not the way of it. He knew it from the detailed coherence of the signals picked up by the radiotelescope. The creature which had saved them was no more

God than Man is God. Cameron had studied enough of physic
to understand that however far Man might penetrate into the
scheme of things, layer upon layer, he would reach no ultimate
truth. Cameron knew the people leaving the cathedral, however
much they might intone their prayers and prostrate themselves,
would never reach God. Even the creature who had reached
out and saved them could never do that, for there was order on
order in infinite progression. Cameron got to his feet. With a
long sigh he made his way slowly into the town.

73 74 75 76 77 10 9 8 7 6 5 4 3 2 1